Nov...
Har...
rom...
by Ann...
comes to life
on the movie screen

starring
KEIR DULLEA · SUSAN PENHALIGON

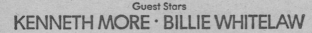

Leopard
in the
Snow

Guest Stars
KENNETH MORE · BILLIE WHITELAW

featuring GORDON THOMSON as MICHAEL
and JEREMY KEMP as BOLT

Produced by JOHN QUESTED and CHRIS HARROP
Screenplay by ANNE MATHER and JILL HYEM
Directed by GERRY O'HARA
An Anglo-Canadian Co-Production

The Shadow Between

by

ANNE HAMPSON

Harlequin Books

TORONTO • LONDON • NEW YORK • AMSTERDAM • SYDNEY

Original hardcover edition published in 1977
by Mills & Boon Limited

ISBN 0-373-02160-7

Harlequin edition published April 1978

PRINTED IN U.S.A.

CHAPTER ONE

THE girl swung around as the door of the elegantly-furnished drawing-room was opened, and a ready smile lit her large, grey-green eyes. She had been arranging flowers in a silver vase and she still held a deep red rose in her hand.

'What a beautiful picture you make, my love.' The man, small of stature but broad and robust, stood in the doorway and admired the dainty, slender girl who was his only child. 'It was all worth while; you've grown up into a gracious lady, and on the day you marry into the nobility my cup will be full.' He came forward, and she lowered her head so that he would miss the frown that had creased her wide, intelligent forehead. If only he would not dream so! To him nothing had ever been impossible, but this latest ambition could never materialise simply because she would never have the opportunity which, to her doting father, seemed so very simple. Besides, she was already in love, *and* with a gentleman of the nobility, though her father had no idea of this.

'Have you finished all your work, Father?' Vicky twisted the rose by its stem, holding it to her nose. 'If so, perhaps we can go to town? I have some shopping to do.'

'We shall certainly go to town if you want to, my pet. You could have driven in yourself, of course.' He smiled at her, then went over to finger one of the roses she had set in the vase. 'What does it feel like to be a driver? My, but I was so proud when you passed your test the first time! Take after your old dad—with nothing allowed to beat you!'

She gave him a lovely smile, watching for a moment as he stood back to admire the flowers.

'I was certainly thrilled when I passed. However, I shan't feel confident until I've had some experience. And I'll not have experience in the Rolls, Father. Please may I have a small car?' The voice, musical and pleading, caused the man to wince a little.

'Darling, you shall have whatever you want. I ought to have known the Rolls would frighten you, although I did like the idea of your driving it. It's a status symbol of which your old dad's exceedingly proud.'

Status symbol ... So many status symbols, thought Vicky, but she only laughed to herself. Her father was like a little boy and every new toy delighted him. He had worked so hard all his life, declaring, when he was no more than fourteen years of age, that he would one day be a millionaire. The fact that he had been born in the slums daunted him not at all, any more than did his lack of an education.

His lovely young wife had died in giving birth to Vicky and Wallace Fraser had never recovered from his loss. But he had adored his daughter and even though he had been working every hour he could, scraping together the money to build his first house, he had willingly spared the cash for a nurse for his baby.

'Just you bring her up right,' he had said to the woman he had eventually chosen from among a dozen or more. 'One day she'll be the daughter of a millionaire!'

The first house was sold long before it was completed, and the second and third. Wallace Fraser was even then building a name as well as his houses. He was such a stickler for perfection that he had been known to order the complete stripping of a bathroom or a kitchen if the fittings had not been put in with the infinite care which he himself would have used. Success was inevitable, but although the rewards came fairly quickly, his ambition to become a millionaire did not come to fruition until he was fifty-four, by which time his daughter was seventeen. And now, at eighteen, she had learned of her father's latest ambition.

'I'm a self-made man, a raw diamond,' he had said. 'But my little girl's been educated properly, and she's a beautiful lady—a lady of quality—No, my precious, don't interrupt me. I have only one ambition left: that my lovely daughter shall marry and become the mistress of a stately home. If a title should go with it so much the better, but I shan't be too disappointed if you aren't addressed as "my lady", since not all the upper classes have titles. It's of no consequence so long as you become the wife of an aristocrat.'

'Father,' protested Vicky, 'please forget such dreams. I'm only *me*—your daughter. The nobility marry their own kind, really they do.'

'These days they go for money, and I have money! I'll settle a fortune on you if need be!' He wagged a forefinger at her. 'Look how many of the so-called rich are having to close up their big houses, or give them away to the National Trust. One day Vicky, my dream will come true!'

She gave a sigh, wondering how she could convince him of her unsuitability to the role of mistress of a stately home. In any case, she had no wish to be married for what her father could settle on her! That kind of contract was outdated a long time ago! However, Vicky made no mention of this as she said,

'Many of your dreams have come true, I admit, but this one can't.' Her thoughts had flown to the man who, almost a year ago, had stolen her heart without knowing

it. He did not live far away, just over the hill, in a lovely
house called Whitethorn Manor. Recently there had been
talk of an impending engagement between Richard Sherrand and Louisa Austin, a beautiful girl whose lineage was
as noble as his, although it was said that her family's great
wealth was a thing of the past, her father now being forced
to sell much of his estate in Shropshire. Richard Sherrand's estate was in Derbyshire, occupying a major part of
the beautiful valley of the Whitethorn River, tributary of
the Derwent. The lovely modern bungalow which Wallace Fraser had built for his daughter and himself was
also in the Whitethorn Valley. Occupying a delightful
situation on a rise above the river, it stood in five acres of
landscaped gardens with, beyond these, several paddocks
and a great area of rough woodland. Vicky, whose excellent taste had been influential in creating an interior
of extraordinary beauty without being in any way flashy
or giving the impression of extreme wealth, was happy
in her home and desired nothing more than that she
she should continue to share it with her father for many
years to come. She would never marry, she had told herself even while admitting to a more sensible view in that
she was very young and might, with time, come to forget
the handsome but austere master of Whitethorn Manor.

For the present, though, this man occupied her
thoughts for long periods at a time and she wondered
what her ambitious parent would think were he to know
how foolish she had been. It was not as if she and Richard Sherrand had ever met; she had glimpsed him first
when she was rambling around, taking stock of the new
territory into which she was soon to move, the bungalow
being almost completed. She had been resting a while
by the gurgling, silver stream, watching its sparkling
waters rushing over some rapids before flowing more
sedately towards the confluence where it would join the

Derwent, when suddenly a movement caught her attention and she looked up. Through the trees she saw a man, tall and distinguished with dark brown hair and an angular face, bronzed and aristocratic. Something strange had stirred within her and she had believed at first that it was fear, as undoubtedly she was trespassing, since her father's land ended at the brand new fence made unobtrusively of rustic poles. Vicky had thought nothing of stooping under the fence, her object being to take a look at that part of the stream which was denied to her father. Richard Sherrand was the owner of the land on which the bungalow had been built, and Vicky could only think that they had been very fortunate indeed in procuring the land.

It never for one moment occurred to her that the apparently wealthy Richard Sherrand might be in dire financial difficulties, and therefore had been forced to sell some of his land.

The second occasion on which Vicky saw Richard was at a local fair, but again he had not noticed her. There was no reason why he should, since she was merely one of a crowd who had come to support the cause for which the fair was given: the provision of a sports centre in the nearby small town of Wellsover. The girl Louisa had been with Richard, and Vicky told her father afterwards that she had never seen a more beautiful young woman.

'Well, I have,' was his instant rejoinder as he gave her one of his familiar fond and appraising looks. 'There isn't anyone around these parts to beat you, my precious! You've your mother's eyes, soft and tender but able to laugh. You've your mother's shining russet-gold hair, her pretty little turned-up nose—*retroussé*, the educated call it, which I suppose is rather more refined than "turned-up", isn't it?'

He was laughing with his merry brown eyes, eyes that often seemed overshadowed by the extraordinarily bushy brows above them. By no means could Wallace Fraser be described as handsome, yet his beautiful young wife had adored him, just as he had adored her. And all the love which he would have lavished on his wife through the years—years of scheming and struggling to achieve his aim—had been lavished on his daughter instead. Yet she had never been spoiled; Wallace was ever watchful of that, wisely aware that a spoiled child is an unhappy one, simply because its selfishness breeds dislike among its acquaintances. So there had been an element of strictness in Vicky's upbringing that had resulted in her having a great respect for her father, but also a certain diffidence which, someone once said, could result in her being 'put on' as she grew older. At this suggestion Wallace had retorted, in his homely, Lancashire voice,

'There's no fear of that while I'm around. I'd protect my girlie with my life.'

The third time Vicky had seen Richard she knew that her heart was affected, and this time her fear was very real, as she knew that her feelings for him would be sure to bring her pain. He had been riding a beautiful stallion across one of his fields; Vicky was on the edge of the wood, looking for wild violets for her father's desk. It was his birthday, and this was one of those little extra touches that had always seemed so endearing to her father.

Richard Sherrand had stopped, dismounted, and began to stroll towards the wood, his own land ending where it began. Here there was no fencing and as she watched his expression, from her hiding-place among the thick foliage of some bushes, Vicky noticed a sudden frown come to his forehead. Something had vexed him, but what? Perhaps, she mused, he was regretting having sold some of his land. Vicky thought that she herself would not care to sell her land if she owned an estate as large and compact as that surrounding Whitethorn Manor. Richard had remained in her vision for a long while; he had seemed to be lost in thought, brooding and upset. Vicky recalled how concerned she had been, wishing she could go out there, revealing herself and asking him what was the matter. But that was impossible. In any case, Richard Sherrand was not the kind of man to approach without an introduction. It was known that he was haughty, that he had all the aristocrat's pride in his ancestry, in the fact of his being one of those favoured people whom the lower strata term 'them' as opposed to 'us'.

Vicky, unlike her father, was ever conscious of her origin, of the fact that her grandmother had been one of those Lancashire lassies referred to by Richard Hoggart. She had been proud but very poor, had brought up five sons and four daughters in a four-roomed terrace house where the 'bathroom' was the shallow brown kitchen sink. Wallace, though ready to own to his background, had now decided that money was what counted in these changed times and therefore he could rise above his past and be respected for his success. Vicky knew this was not so; she had been taught well by her nurse, then her governess, and then she had gone to a good school, so she was more conversant with the ways of those people with whom her father so optimistically believed she could be classed as equal. Vicky's school friends had come from higher walks of life than she ... and they had often let her see this, despite the fact that they could not help but like her, so charming was her personality.

'My child ...' Wallace's quiet voice came to Vicky and

her musings ceased as she smiled at him across the room, the rose still in her hand. 'What daydreams are running around in that head of yours?'

'Father,' she returned seriously, 'please don't get these impossible ideas about me. I wasn't dreaming of a handsome prince riding over that hill there and claiming me as his bride.'

The man standing there was silent for a space, his eyes a little frowning in their deep sockets. At last he looked directly at her and said almost aggressively,

'I've never set my heart on anything and failed in my desire! I shan't fail now! I've only one ambition left, as you know, and that's to see my girl as the wife of a nobleman. I want the setting for your beauty; I want what in my opinion you are fitted for! I've worked for the making of money and I'll not deny that I've had more luck than most, what with being recognised by those with the money to build miniature palaces, and then being given so many public buildings. Yes, I've been lucky, but on the other hand I've never been afraid of work. When you were small, love, I used to work for as much as eighteen hours a day. Well, that's all over and done with now; others do the work while I merely govern from this office I have here.' He stopped, watching Vicky as she bent over the vase to place the last rose into the arrangement she had so charmingly made. 'I want to see my girl mixing with the highest in the land! Vicky, I *shall* have you married to someone who really is someone!'

She gave a small sigh, yet her expression was sweet and smiling. What pleasure such a marriage would give her father! But why did he not admit, once and for all, that his dream held no substance, that there was no handsome aristocrat just around the corner who would suddenly appear, take one look at Vicky, and declare that she was the girl for him?

She stood for a moment looking at her flower arrangement, and then, walking slowly to her father, she slipped a hand into his and, turning her head, kissed him on the cheek.

'I love you,' she said simply. 'You must be the most wonderful father in the whole world!'

'And you the most wonderful daughter. Do you know, love, that for those first few days after your mother had died I almost hated you? My beloved had given her life for that tiny babe lying there ... and I thought to myself, "I wish she had died instead." But after the funeral, when you were crying there, so lonely in your cot, I stood and looked down, and—and I thought how very helpless you were. Vicky, my love, I suddenly knew that I could give you all that I would have given you dear mother ...'

His voice faltered in spite of the smile he had forced to his lips. Vicky twisted around, and put her strong young arms about him, gently fingering away the great tear that had rolled unashamedly down his cheek. Her heart swelled with love for him, and she thought how unfair it was that he had lost his wife after less than a year of marriage. 'You're growing more like her every day,' he continued when presently he collected himself. 'She had such a dainty figure, and flawless complexion. Her mouth was wide and generous, and red as that rose you just had in your hand.' His voice was gruff but his face had lost its momentary look of grief. Vicky thought that all she would ever want would be his happiness, and if only he would put aside that absurd dream of his then there would be nothing of any great importance that could possibly stand in the way of his complete contentment.

A month went by and Vicky was beginning to dread the mention of her probable marriage to a man of quality.

She racked her brain to find some way of destroying her father's ambition without hurting him too much. She tried to explain that she was perfectly happy here with him; she pointed out that she was still very young for marriage, that he would be lonely when she left the home he had so recently built for them, but it was all to no avail. He seemed obsessed by his desire, but at the same time was unable to launch Vicky into that kind of society where she would meet the people he had in mind. Once or twice he had contrived to gain an invitation to some special dinner, but he had seemed like a square peg in a round hole, being almost totally ignored by the people he so wanted to cultivate. Vicky, her heart aching for him, tried again to make him see sense.

'Just look at all these beatiful girls,' she had said, flinging out a hand indicatingly. 'They're the daughters and sisters of titled men; they are the ones who will be chosen, not anyone like me with no proper background.'

'What does background matter?' he had demanded, at which Vicky had been quick to point out his own admission that it meant a great deal.

'Because otherwise,' she added gently, 'you'd not be so anxious for me to marry into the nobility, would you?'

'You're trying to muddle me,' he had protested, aggrieved. 'I know what I want, child—and I shall get what I want!'

About a week later Vicky went off, to wander over the wild moorlands and into the valleys of tiny mountain streams. It was late spring and the sun was shining on the hills, glistening on the cascade that fell from Dimtor down into the river far below; it painted the clouds with gold, and the harsh outcrops with a soft amber-yellow.

It was so good to be alive! Vicky, the breeze in her hair and on her face, strode out, her neck arched, her eyes on the distant mountains. And then, out of the deep silence, there came a sound and she swung about, not knowing what to expect.

Richard Sherrand ...

He was walking by the stream, his head bent. Vicky stood still on the bank, waiting for him to pass. But he stopped, his arrogant eyes flickering over her and appearing to take in every single thing about her—her figure, clad in a white pleated skirt and rollneck sweater, her face, glowing with health, her russet-gold hair, styled in a page-boy bob and gleaming in the sunlight. For the first time she saw him at close quarters, and it was with a little quickening of surprise that she saw just how formidable his countenance was. Lean and darkly bronzed, its lines severely etched as if in stone, it gave the impression of ruthlessness amounting almost to cruelty. The nose had an aquiline quality, the mouth seemed far too thin. The jaw, flexed as if permanently rigid, matched the outthrust chin to perfection, as did the high, prominent cheekbones with their hollows underneath. Vicky was frowning inwardly, for she had not noticed this excessive austerity before, nor the harshness which seemed to pervade the man's whole being. He was different ... Still handsome, but not as handsome as before.

She looked into his eyes and decided they were grey, like granite and as hard. His hair was thick and wavy and, at the present moment, teased by the wind. Vicky's chief emotion was one of disappointment; she wondered what had happened to that rather full mouth, which she had had to admit was faintly sensual, and where was that lazy expression which she had thought to be so attractive? She had seen his face softened by a laugh when he had been talking to Louisa Austin, had noticed the long-lashed eyes—which at the time she had believed to be dark blue—look tenderly into the face of the girl at his side.

'You're Miss Fraser?' The voice was low and cultured, but somehow Vicky detected a discordant note in it, a sort of rasping tone which came as a complete surprise to her. She nodded her head, shyness holding her in its grip for a moment so that she had difficulty in articulating words. But at last she did manage to say yes, she was Miss Fraser. 'Your father bought some of my land.' He seemed to give a sigh, and his mouth twisted as though he were in some sort of pain, either physical or mental. Vicky strongly suspected that it was the latter.

'Yes, he did. We're very pleased with our house and its wonderful setting.' She was wanting to keep him, but also wanting to say something that would erase that brooding expression from his face.

'You should be.' His grey eyes wandered, to the hill over which the bungalow had been built. 'Your father has a nice place there.'

'We had an excellent architect.'

'So it would appear.' Unexpected bitterness edged his voice. 'There are just the two of you, I'm told?'

'Yes, that's right.' She smiled up into his face, profoundly conscious that he attracted her in spite of his austerity. Every nerve in her body seemed to be tingling, and her heart was beating far too quickly for comfort. 'My mother died when I was born.'

He looked at her with a little more interest, as if he were dwelling upon her words.

'That's very sad. Your father brought you up, then?'

She nodded, surprised that he should be talking to her like this. Vicky had heard it said that he was a snob, considering himself far above the *nouveau riche* who were nowadays managing to live the good life hitherto reserved for the privileged few.

'It was very difficult for him, since he had so much

work to do. He had a nanny for me at first, and then a governess.'

The grey eyes flickered.

'You were fortunate,' he remarked.

'Yes, indeed. People of our status didn't employ nannies for their children. I went to school later, of course.' Vicky was happy, inordinately so. Never in her wildest dreams had she envisaged talking like this to the man who had had such an effect on her emotions that she felt she would never be able to forget him—no, not even when he was married to the beautiful Louisa.

'And now you just stay at home with your father?'

'I run the house,' answered Vicky demurely. 'We have servants, of course, but I like to do some of the jobs myself. I always choose what we shall have for meals,' she went on to confide. 'It's fun, trying out new things to eat.'

She thought she saw the shade of a smile touch his lips, thought his eyes had softened slightly and his face seemed definitely to relax. Nevertheless, he was cool, speaking to her with a sort of impersonal detachment as he said,

'You dine at home most of the time, then?'

'Sometimes we go out, but I prefer our cosy dinners at home. Father still works fairly hard, being in his office for the greater part of the day, and I feel it's relaxing for him to dine at home.'

A small silence followed before Richard spoke.

'I'll bid you good day, Miss Fraser. Remember me to your father.'

'I will.' Her beautiful eyes met his, and she was suddenly bewildered by the strange expression she saw there. 'Goodbye, Mr Sherrand.' Her voice was low, and faintly dejected. It had been a wonderful few minutes ... and now it was all over ...

'Goodbye.' Turning on his heel, he strode away in the direction from which he had come. He would keep to the river bank, she knew, and this would eventually lead him to the back entrance of his lovely home, a home which had been declared to be one of the best existing examples of medieval architecture in England. In structure it resembled Haddon Hall, which was also in Derbyshire, but some distance from Whitethorn Manor. Vicky knew from local gossip that the Manor was very old, having been described, even before the end of the sixteenth century, as '*auncient*, strong, large and faire'. She had learned too of the treasures which abounded within the stout walls—beautiful antique furniture and porcelain, priceless tapestries and carpets, to say nothing of the renowned collection of weapons, many of which adorned the high walls of the main hall of the Manor. There were halberds, battleaxes, pikes, swords, pistols and many others. Suits of armour stood on the floor, their breastplates shining; huge urns were filled with flowers, just to soften the austerity of the numerous weapons of war.

When she arrived back at the bungalow Vicky told her father about her meeting with their neighbour.

'He actually spoke to me,' she told him, her face flushed and her eyes sparkling. 'He seems stern and rather distant, but he wasn't as haughty with me as I expected.'

'He wasn't?' Wallace Fraser's brown eyes held a strange expression. 'Tell me, child, what *did* he say to you?'

She looked at him in some surprise, for he appeared to be quite unnecessarily curious about the meeting she had had with the Lord of the Manor of Whitethorn.

'He asked about us—if we lived alone. He didn't seem to know that Mother had died and that you and I were on our own here.'

'No . . .' A silent moment passed before Wallace added to this one softly-spoken word. 'The business of the land was done mainly through the agent—and the lawyers, of course. But Richard Sherrand and I did meet on a couple of occasions. I found him somewhat arrogant and superior in his dealings with me and it was plain that he considered my type of Croesus to be far beneath him.' Wallace's mouth curved in a smile, a smile which held no resentment whatsoever. 'My money was filthy lucre, whereas his was the untarnished inheritance handed down to him through a succession of illustrious ancestors.' Again he was silent and Vicky made no attempt to interrupt his thoughts. 'There's a difference according to these people; for myself I fail to see any difference at all.'

She looked affectionately at him, noting the way the knot of his tie had slipped to one side of his collar, how his shirt was a little rumpled at the front where it showed between the lapels of his coat. The aristocratic Richard Sherrand would never look like this, she decided. Yet what did it matter? It was what lay beneath the covering that was really important.

'Perhaps the wealthy can't accustom themselves to the dramatic change in our society,' she murmured after a while. 'It wouldn't be fair to judge them, Father. They've been brought up in a different world from the one you were brought up in.' Again she looked at him, freely admitting that no matter what he did to himself, no matter what sort of clothes he wore, he could never look the gentleman. In his own words he was a rough diamond . . . but she loved him dearly. His heart was in the right place and always had been, for even in that frenzied race to reach his objective he had always been able to spare a few pounds for anyone less fortunate than himself.

'Yes, that's true. But you, my precious, were brought up properly. You're a lady——'

'I'm your daughter,' she interrupted him gently. 'That's far more important to me than being a lady.'

'Well said, my dearest child.' There was no doubt that her words had given him infinite pleasure. 'What a treasure you've been to me! I'm glad I worked so hard, glad that I've become a millionaire——' He stopped abruptly, as if deciding that he ought not to keep on mentioning this fact. 'Tell me some more about our neighbour,' he said invitingly. 'How was he with you?'

'As I said, he wasn't as haughty as I would have expected. You know how people talk, how we've heard that he's a snob. Well, he was very civil, though cool in his manner of speaking. I think those people usually are cool and—sort of—er—distant towards people like me——'

'He's no need to be!' Anger edged Wallace's voice and his brown eyes glinted beneath their absurdly bushy brows. 'You, my child, are far——' He broke off, frowning and shaking his head. 'Go on,' he urged. 'You were saying he was civil to you.'

'He said it was very sad that my mother had died, and spoke about your bringing me up. I explained how difficult it had been for you because you were working so hard. I told him I had a nanny, then a governess.'

Wallace listened intently, seeming to hang on every word. Vicky, never having noticed a mood like this before, found herself bewildered by it. She had often seen him in a calculating mood, often before some big deal he was hoping to pull off, or some new investment he was about to make, but this was different, and in any case, he had now given up making big deals, having decided that he could relax and enjoy to some extent the money he had made.

'Did he seem surprised by the fact that you were a real lady?'

Vicky's eyes opened wide.

'What makes you ask a question like that?' she wanted to know.

He shrugged, as if to bring the conversation down to one of a mere casual interchange, but Vicky knew him far too well to be deceived.

Her father was contemplaing something ... But what?

'I just had the idea that he might be surprised that I, a rough Lancashire man with an accent that would give me away as soon as I opened my mouth, should have a daughter as refined and ladylike as you.'

'Father,' said Vicky sternly, 'please stop belittling yourself. I assure you I wasn't in the least interested in any comparisons he might be making—though I feel sure he had no such thing in mind,' she added, more for herself than for her father. She hated the idea that Richard Sherrand should look down on her father, and wanted to think he was far above anything so petty.

'You do?' Wallace, shrewd as always, suddenly became interested in the slight flush that had come to his daughter's cheeks. 'What else did he say to you, my love?' The brown eyes were wide, observant, but Vicky, with no notion that he was trying to read her thoughts, freely related what had passed between her and Richar Sherrand, all unknowing that the flush had increased, that her eyes had become dreamy yet tinged with a wistfulness that was most revealing to the man sitting there, his mind alert ... and darting to the future.

'He asked to be remembered to you,' ended Vicky, her memory taking her back to the tinge of dejection she had experienced when those precious few minutes she had spent with Richard were over.

'He did? That was thoughtful of him,' mused Wallace. 'Yes, very thoughtful of him ...'

Frowning, Vicky asked him why he was so preoccupied.

'You're so strange today,' she chided, but gently. 'I've never seen you in a mood like this before.'

He shook his head from side to side.

'I've never been in a mood like this before,' he confessed. 'There hasn't been an occasion to fit it,' he added cryptically, and his daughter's frown deepened.

'I won't have you keeping secrets,' she told him severely. 'Come clean and tell me what's on your mind.'

He laughed, then, and cast her an affectionate glance.

'I'm merely talking to myself,' he confessed. 'You should be used to that by now.' He paused a moment in thought before saying, 'I have a telephone call to make, love.' His voice was so deceivingly casual that Vicky never even thought of asking him whom he was calling. 'So if you'll excuse me. Oh, and by the way, go and see that Amazon in the kitchen, who terrifies me but is putty in your hands, and get her to excel herself with the cooking tonight; we might be having a guest. If we don't then the cooking won't be wasted on you and me, my love, so do see that she produces something rather special.' And before Vicky could even open her mouth to ask who the visitor was her father had opened the door and disappeared through it.

She had to laugh despite her curiosity and bewilderment. He was no different from when he was making momentous decisions; action—immediate action—was all-important to success, he had always maintained. But this time it was no business deal he was contemplating . . . or was it?

CHAPTER TWO

THE table had never looked so inviting and as she stood back surveying her handiwork Vicky could not help feeling proud of the artistry which she had employed in the flower arrangements, the positioning of the candelabra, the intricate folding of the hand-embroidered napkins. The silver was Georgian, the glass hand-engraved, the porcelain late eighteenth-century Derby.

'Well, my child, are you happy with your two hours' hard work?' Wallace had come to stand beside his daughter and his hand slid about her shoulders. 'It looks too nice to disturb!'

She turned, leaning against him, her face creased in a frown of puzzlement.

'I can't think why you should want to invite Mr Sherrand to our house, Father. Even less do I understand how he came to accept your invitation. You won't admit that you're contemplating a business deal with him, but something tells me that you are.'

To her surprise he laughed at this, as though it had some connection with a private joke of his.

'It's a social occasion, my dear,' he began, but Vicky instantly interrupted him, pulling away and subjecting him to a look of censure.

'You tell fibs,' she accused. 'Mr Sherrand isn't used to paying friendly visits to our kind of people.'

'Our kind?' For a brief moment Wallace's mouth was tight. 'You, Vicky, have nothing to be ashamed of. Why do you suppose I started right at the beginning, providing a nanny who'd had experience with the wealthy, the nobility? Then your governess—she'd worked for an earl and his wife. And the school I sent you to. You mixed with the élite, the cream of society. No, dear, you must never consider yourself beneath anyone—*anyone*, do you understand? Richard Sherrand isn't above you, not by any means. In fact, it might interest you to know that he, like all his kind, is suffering from the changes which are taking place in our economy.'

There was a strange pause during which Vicky, her eyes fixed upon her father's face, tried to fathom just what was in his mind. Inevitably it had occurred to her that he might have settled his eye on Richard Sherrand as a likely husband for her, but the idea had been dismissed instantly. Her father knew that Richard was almost engaged to Louisa Austin and therefore was not 'eligible' any more.

'I expect our guest will secretly be envying us our secure financial position,' Wallace was saying. 'I depend on industry while he merely has the income from the estate. That house must be a tremendous drain on his resources and, like so many more of the aristocracy, he's had to cut down drastically on the number of servants he employs. There used to be ten gardeners up at the Manor; today there are two. In the house Richard's father had no fewer than twenty-two servants: maids, footmen, a butler and a valet. Today there are only four servants to keep that vast place in order. Why, *we* have three—with that genius in the kitchen, that is. And we have three gardeners, and could have even more——'

'Father,' Vicky could not help interrupting, 'how do you come to know all this?'

He seemed to colour slightly, but Vicky could not be sure.

'I heard it at odd times from——' He stopped to flip a careless hand. 'From one or other of the village gossips.'

She looked suspiciously at him.

'You never talk to the gossips,' she said.

'One hears things, my love.' Wallace eyed the table again. 'As I was saying, it looks far too attractive to spoil. You've excelled yourself this time and no mistake.'

She said nothing, but glanced at the clock. Richard Sherrand coming here ... When her father first told her she had been rather stunned, unable to believe that the exalted owner of Whitethorn Manor would condescend to come to diner with her father and herself. She had asked her father what he was about, whether he had some special reason for inviting Richard Sherrand to their home, but he had been evasive, and had even spoken sharply to her on one occasion, successfully putting an end to her questions. She had gone back to the kitchen, to help Grace with such things as sauces and garnishings for the roast duckling which was to be served on a silver tray, after the starter of smoked salmon. The fish course which Grace wanted to include had been dispensed with by Vicky, who always thought that too many courses spoiled any meal, whether it be dinner or merely lunch. The sweet which Grace had made was one of her many specialities: strawberry meringue, with the strawberries topped by fresh clotted cream and chopped walnuts.

'I think it's time I went and got ready,' she said into the silence which had fallen on the dining-room as she and her father stood there, admiring the table. 'It'll take me rather longer than usual,' she added with a grimace.

'Yes, my dear, do take extra care, won't you? Not that you don't always look charming, but tonight is rather special, our guest being who he is.' Wallace, by avoiding Vicky's eyes, was doing something he had never done before, and at the same time adding to her perplexity.

Well, she decided, she must surely soon know what it was all about, since if her father and Mr Sherrand were considering a business deal together then they would obviously talk about it at the dinner table.

After taking a bath Vicky put on dainty underwear and then a dress of white embroidered tulle with a layered skirt and low-cut neckline bordered with a narrow silver ribbon on which were set, about four inches apart, star-shaped diamanté studs. An antique silver necklace fitting tightly around her throat, and a matching pair of ear-rings were all the jewellery Vicky decided to wear, though she literally had boxes full of jewellery which her father had bought her during the past few years. Both the neck-lace and earrings were very plain, as was her hair-style, being set in the pageboy bob, but with a fringe rather than the flipped-up curl which she usually preferred.

A glance in the mirror more than satisfied her, but she added a little colour to her lips for all that, and of course there was the final use of the perfume spray, and the tucking of a dainty lace handkerchief into the tightly-buttoned cuff of her dress.

Would Richard like her dress? Would he appreciate the expensive perfume? Vicky was soon chiding herself for these questions, keeping in mind both the difference in their social status and, even more important, the fact that he was probably already engaged to the beautiful and glamorous Louisa Austin—although no announce-ment had yet been made so far as Vicky knew.

Wallace, looking well and fit and very smart in his dinner jacket and immaculate white shirt with its ruching down the front, was waiting for her in the sitting-room. Dusk was approaching, but it was not yet time to put on the lights. Vicky, as always at this time, was interested in the scene outside—the gardens with their lovely trees, many of which, being part of the estate, were hundreds of years old—the flowering bushes which had been planted at a stage of maturity and so were looking as if they had been established for much longer than they had. The lawns were like velvet, immaculate and not a blade of grass out of place. The summer-house nestled snugly within a delightful arbour, the swimming-pool, though some distance from the house, was still a very attractive adjunct to the overall scene of beauty which the grounds offered to those who appreciated the combined handiwork of man and nature.

Vicky sighed contentedly and thought how fortunate she was to be living in such a lovely setting, a setting which was part of an ancient estate, the demesne lands of a man whose first ancestors had come over with the Conqueror.

'Let me look at you.' Wallace put out his hands and touched his daughter's shoulders, fingering the earrings and then the necklace.

'It was your dear mother's set,' he murmured, and Vicky said nothing because she knew he was in the distant past, with the wife he had adored, the wife who died when she was only two years older than Vicky was now. 'I bought it for her wedding-present and it was very cheap, really. This sort of thing was cheap in those days ...' The big brown eyes were vacant, and in them Vicky saw a hint of moisture that brought a certain mistiness to her own eyes.

'That's why I wore it tonight.' Vicky spoke as her father stepped back, the better to look upon her slender, white-clad figure. 'Because it was Mother's. I wear this set only on special occasions, you know.'

He nodded slowly.

'It's as it should be ... tonight you should be wearing this particular set.'

Vicky gave a sigh but made no comment; questions

seemed out of place, somehow, at this time, and in any case, her father was still a long way from her ... with her mother, and even she, Vicky, had no right to intrude into the memories he was obviously calling back.

It was the bell that brought him back from his reverie. He looked his daughter over again, as if assuring himself that everything about her was perfect.

One of the maids went to the door, with Wallace moving into the hall. Vicky, standing just inside the living-room, heard her father's cordial greeting, and the quieter, more cultured voice of his guest. Vicky's heart gave a little jerk, and it seemed that every nerve was rioting. Her feelings became mixed; she wondered one moment if the evening would be an ordeal, yet the next moment her whole being was filled with pleasurable anticipation. She would have Richard's company for several hours ... Her eyes glowed suddenly, and her soft lips quivered tremulously. And it was at this moment that Richard entered the room, to see her standing there, very unsure of herself, yet alluringly attractive in her white dress, the simple necklace and earrings catching the light which had now been switched on.

'Good evening,' he said graciously. 'We meet again very soon, Miss Fraser.'

'Good evening,' she murmured. 'Please sit down.' Her father was watching her and she knew she must not let him down. Because he had gone to so much trouble to ensure her becoming a 'lady' he naturally expected her to know all there was to know about etiquette. However, he himself asked Richard what he would like to drink, then went over to the cocktail cabinet to get it. Richard sat down, taking the chair indicated to him by Vicky. His grey eyes rested on her face for a long moment before moving to the lovely curve of her neck, and then to her breasts, small, firm, immature. She lowered her lashes, embarrassed by his stare and the fact that it was totally unsmiling. That austerity which she had decided amounted to a harshness she had not noticed at first was strongly in evidence now, and she knew a tinge of dejection, wishing she could say something that would erase it from his otherwise handsome features.

The two men chatted, but with a reserve that made Vicky wonder if her father had specifically requested Richard not to discuss the object of his visit in front of his daughter. Vicky, content to listen, and to watch Richard's every change of expression, sat comfortably in her chair, sipping her drink. Richard was saying, in answer to a question her father had put to him,

'I suppose you *could* use the word "venerable" to describe the Manor. The guide books always do.'

'It must be gratifying to have a home which is so old, which has been passed from father to son over so many centuries.'

'One becomes so used to the idea that it slips the memory. You just live your life like anyone else.'

'You must have a certain pride, though,' persisted Wallace. 'I believe you have the actual suit of armour which one of your ancestors wore at the Battle of Rowton Moor?'

Faintly Richard smiled; it was plainly a smile of bitterness.

'Yes, I have.'

'It's to be hoped that all your treasures can remain intact. I always consider it a tragedy when homes like yours are sold up and their precious contents taken off by foreigners—for that's what's happening today. We're losing all our antiques to collectors abroad.'

Vicky, not at all pleased by what her father was saying, since it was tactless to say the least, could not help but catch the spasm of pain that crossed their visitor's

face. Surely his home was not in danger? Her father had
been saying that many wealthy landowners were in difficulty, and had even suggested that Richard was the
same, making a point of the major reduction in his staff.
Even so, Vicky could not imagine an estate like Whitethorn ever coming under the auctioneer's hammer. Apart
from owning three villages and other property, Richard
owned about fifty farms in the county, and his own home
farm covered something like a thousand acres. Yet she
heard him say that few estates of the size of Whitethorn
remained intact these days. Then he stopped abruptly,
as if he considered himself above discussing his home
with a man like Wallace Fraser.

He lifted his glass, turning it slowly as he watched the
amber-coloured liquid catching and reflecting the light
from the subtly shaded wall lamps above his head. Vicky
could not take her eyes off his profile, so distinguished
it was, with those clear-cut lines, that thoroughly mascu-
line mouth and chin, that aquiline nose and clear forehead above which his hair shone, clean and appearing
lighter than it was owing to the angle of the lamps whose
glow was cast upon it. She thought of Louisa Austin
and a sigh escaped her. How lucky the girl was, winning
the love of a man like Richard Sherrand. Vicky hoped
that Louisa was a 'nice' girl, that she was deserving of a
man as handsome and rich as the owner of Whitethorn
Manor. At the thought that Louisa might not be worthy
of Richard Vicky's blood seemed to become chilled, as
if crystals of ice had formed in her veins.

She supposed she had paled a little, for her father,
glancing sideways at her, said swiftly, and with anxiety
in his voice,

'Are you all right, dear? You don't look quite yourself.'

She smiled at once, throwing off her absurd mind-wanderings,

'Of course. I'll go and see how dinner's getting on. I've an idea we ought to be moving into the dining-room.' She turned to Richard as she rose from the chair. 'Please excuse me,' she said graciously, and left the room. No sooner had she closed the door than she heard her father say, a briskness in his voice that startled her, so different was it from the tones he had used up till now,

'Well, seeing that I've sent out feelers to you once or twice, there's no need for any wasted words. If you can take to the idea ...' Vicky heard no more, as she had moved on. But she frowned as she went to the kitchen, her mind on her father's words. That he had some scheme in mind was certain, and she was frustrated at being kept in the dark as to what it was. Wallace had never deliberately been evasive as he was at present; in fact, he had often discussed his projects with her, so his attitude now was extremely baffling, to say the least.

The dinner was served a short while later, the first course being brought in by one of the maids. Richard, obviously interested in the way the girl served him at the table, seemed to be giving her full marks. Wallace beamed with satisfaction as she made her exit from the room, silently and with a smile for Wallace as she closed the door behind her.

'I've been mighty lucky with my servants, eh?' he said. 'Nothing slovenly about any of them as you see to-day. Of course, the secret's to pay well—over the odds. Then you get the cream.' Wallace picked up his glass and took a drink of his wine. As he returned the glass to its coaster he touched one of the orchids that formed the individual flower decoration that Vicky had placed at the side of each cover. One of the gardeners, an expert

at orchid growing, had already produced some delightful blooms and he was experimenting with some new
strains he had had sent in from the Far East.

Richard made no comment on what his host had said
about servants, but concentrated on his food, appearing
to be enjoying it, but at the same time Vicky had the conviction that he was quickly becoming bored both with her
father and herself. She knew that her father should not be
talking about the quality of his servants, and declaring
that the only way to be sure of efficiency was to pay
higher wages than what was usual. But Richard should
be tolerant, bearing with the man whose background
was so inferior to his own. Richard had had everything
since birth; Wallace had fought and toiled and sweated
for what he had managed to acquire in the way of wealth.
Yes, Richard should be understanding . . . and Vicky felt
sure he could be understanding if only he would give a
little thought to what her father had been through.

When the meal was over Richard politely expressed
his appreciation, and even congratulated Wallace on his
cook. This naturally gratified Wallace and he beamed
upon his guest.

'I'm happy that you've enjoyed it,' he said. 'We'll have
coffee and liqueurs in the lounge—and a cigarette if you
wish. I don't smoke myself and neither does Vicky, but
we never object to others indulging.' He led the way to
the high-ceilinged room to which Richard had at first
been shown. Vicky, glancing round, wondered how Richard was comparing it with some room or other in his own
home. Here, the modern influence prevailed for the most
part, but Vicky, with a flair for decor and an eye for bal-
ance, had created a room of unusual taste and beauty.
The wall lamps were antiques, having once held candles;
the two standard lamps had also held candles originally.
Vicky had had them converted to electricity, although

she still burned many candles, and at this moment the room was lit by candles alone—candles in silver candelabra, in individual candlesticks, in coloured glass funnels placed on various pieces of furniture about the room. They glowed red, green, amber and rose, lending a fairy-tale-like quality to the gracious apartment. All the other rooms in the house were the same, having received a lavish amount of care both in decor and in furnishing. Vicky's bedroom was in coral and white, with satinwood doors and skirting. Her father's room was in deep purple with lilac carpet and drapes. He had wanted darker walls than Vicky's, suggesting he have brown wallpaper. She would not have it, and so they compromised with the purple.

'It's not a man's room!' he had protested, yet had fingered appreciatively the lilac bedspread with its exquisite embroidery. 'In any case, purple's a royal colour, and I'm only one of the rag-tag and bobtail!'

She had laughed merrily, then hugged him and told him he was no such thing.

'You're the best builder in England! The king of builders, so what's wrong with purple?'

'You have an answer for everything, my love. All right, if it pleases you I'll endure it!'

'You'll *enjoy* it, you mean! I've known you too long to be taken in by *that* expression!'

And so every room in the house had received its share of Vicky's planning and now, as she watched Richard, trying to derive some information from his grey eyes as they glanced around, she could not help feeling an access of pride at the achievement. A brilliant architect whom her father had employed many times before, her father's most skilled employees; the infinite care with which the interior had been planned ... all these compounded to produce a home that was as near perfect as any home could be. A firm of landscape gardeners were at work immediately the building plans were passed, so there was no loss in growing time. The house and the gardens were both completed more or less at the same time.

Richard sat down without commenting on the pretty effect which the candles gave, but Vicky somehow knew that he had taken a great deal of notice of everything in the room. He smiled at her as she looked at him from her comfortable place on the couch, and her cup was full even before he said,

'What a pleasant evening this has been. It's so restful here. No wonder you said, Miss Fraser, that you and your father were very pleased with your house and its wonderful setting.'

'We have you to thank for selling us the land,' Wallace was generous enough to remind him.

'I admit I was troubled at the idea of selling. You're the first people to be allowed to build on the estate.' Was there a hint of bitterness again? Vicky wondered. Also, she was puzzled by the words, 'You're the first ...' Was he contemplating selling more land?

The evening came to an end all too soon for Vicky, who had received several more smiles from their guest. And when he was leaving she heard him say,

'You must both come and dine at the Manor. I'll give you a ring, Mr Fraser, and make a definite date.'

'Well——' Wallace rubbed his hands together just as soon as the front door closed upon Richard. 'What a success that was! Tell me, my love, do you like our new friend?'

'I wouldn't go so far as to assume he'll be our friend,' she said warningly. 'I must say, though, I'm pleasantly surprised that he'd invite us to the Manor.'

'Do you like him?' asked her father again.

'Yes, I do.' She looked away, aware of the touch of

colour that had come to her cheeks. Wallace looked at her long and hard, waiting for her to raise her head. This she did eventually, and smiled at him faintly, and tremulously. The evening had been a happy one for her and she would treasure every moment, and especially those smiles which Richard had bestowed upon her. She was aware of looking her best, of carrying off her role of hostess with a fair amount of confidence and a full amount of success. There could be no fault found with anything she did or said. Richard must have been favourably impressed, she thought ... but as yet she did not know just how favourably impressed ...

It was only three days later that Richard telephoned to invite Wallace and Vicky to the Manor. They were to dine with him the following evening, and Wallace insisted that Vicky should buy a new dress for the occasion.

'But I have dozens of dresses,' she protested. 'What on earth do I need another one for?'

'A special occasion, love,' he said, and as she knew from experience just how far she could go in an argument with her father Vicky capitulated and they went together in the car to Sheffield where, for a sum which made even Vicky gasp, a dress of Chinese silk was bought. Of a delicate shade of green, with orange and silver embroidery, and with a mandarin collar and very short sleeves, it was decidedly a model of perfection.

'I shall wear Mother's set again,' she decided, and knew that nothing could have pleased her father more. He bought her shoes and an evening bag to match the dress. She had her hair washed and set while they were in Sheffield because, her father said, there wasn't a really good salon either in their village or in the town in which they usually did their shopping.

She was excited all day and when at last the time came

for her and her father to leave the bungalow in the car she could not understand how she had allowed herself to get in such a state.

'How do you feel, love?' asked her father as they drove along the wide avenue of trees leading to the front fore-court of the Manor. 'Do you realise that at last we are accepted by the aristocracy?'

'By Mr Sherrand,' she corrected, 'not by the aristocracy as a whole.'

'But you will be,' he stated, and there was a hint of defiance in his voice which seemed alien to the confidence with which he continued, 'You'll be a great lady, looked up to by the nobility. They'll respect you, admire you, accept you as one of them!'

She shook her head, sighing a little.

'You don't seem to understand, Father. I'm perfectly happy as we are. I have no ambition to be accepted by the nobility, as you term them.'

'Perfectly happy? But no woman reaches the peak of happiness until she marries the man she loves.'

'One day that might come,' she told him gently, and her thoughts were mainly with Richard, and the hope-lessness of the love that had come to her without her even being aware of it. 'Until then, Father, I'm content to be with you, in our pretty home, with everything a girl can ever want.'

'No! A girl wants marriage and a husband who loves her. She wants a family to care for——'

'And where do you come into this?' Vicky was asking as he brought the car to a standstill on the well-lighted forecourt.

'I'll be around, never fear.'

Vicky made no answer; in any case, the door was be-ing opened by Richard himself who, tall and distin-guished in evening dress, smiled down at Vicky before looking at her father. Her heart gave a great lurch and she found herself tongue-tied for a moment, unable to return his greeting.

The meal was eaten in a very different setting from that of the bungalow, the dining-room of the Manor being a delightful apartment hung with tapestries and rare paintings. The mullioned windows were draped with blue velvet trimmed with gold braid, the fireplace was of marble, with a huge Etruscan vase at either side and in the centre the coat of arms of the Sherrand family. A Buhl table held tureens of silver and priceless porcelain from which the food was served by a manservant whose face was an expressionless mask—very different from the smiling maid who served the dinner at the bungalow! Vicky appreciatively took in such delights as the ormolu vases on a table at the side of the fireplace, the bronzes, and marble busts, the exquisite Limosin enamels and many other rare and precious antiques.

Richard, watching Vicky closely, had an odd expression on his face, and suddenly a frown appeared, as if some distasteful thought had crossed his mind. Vicky, glancing at him, thought she detected a hint of sadness about his eyes, and she could have sworn that he was sighing inwardly. Within seconds the frown was gone and he became the gracious host, anxious that his guests should find everything entirely to their satisfaction.

During the meal the two men talked and Vicky, content to remain quiet, fell to wondering about Richard, about his childhood and his early youth. She knew, from various snippets of information mentioned by one of the gardeners, or one of the maids, that his father had died two years ago, that he had a stepmother who had been so extravagant that quarrels between her and her husband became frequent and in the end they separated, Richard's father having to settle a large sum of money on her as an inducement for her to agree to leave the Manor. Richard had left a few months after the marriage, as he and his stepmother were unable to get along together. After the departure of his stepmother Richard had returned, taking on the management of the estate—which had apparently been much neglected in Richard's absence— when his father's health began to fail.

'Miss Fraser, you're not eating your fish. Is it not to your liking?' Richard's voice, low and cultured and, to Vicky, inordinately attractive, broke into her reverie and she smiled at him, saying yes, the fish was delicious. 'Good. I apologise for my neglect; your father and I were engrossed in something which obviously didn't interest you.'

'That's all right,' returned Vicky. 'I like my own thoughts at times. Please don't trouble about me.'

'But I must,' he smiled. 'Let's change the topic of conversation.' He glanced at Wallace, who nodded instantly. 'Tell me what you think of the Manor, Miss Fraser. You haven't seen much, of course, so I shall invite you over one afternoon and show you round.'

She gave him a look of surprise, her pulses racing. For his expression was no longer one of mere friendliness ... No, there was much more in it than that! He asked again what she thought of his home; she was so shy all at once that she could manage only a stumbling,

'It's—very—beautiful, Mr Sherrand. The—the antiques must be priceless.'

'Not quite,' he returned with a hint of amusement. 'But most of them have a history, which I must relate to you some time.'

Some time ... What did it mean? And why should Richard offer to show her round his home? Not unnaturally Vicky's thoughts bounded on to the possibility of his being interested in her, but immediately there

emerged the picture of Louisa Austin, and Vicky's
bright road to happiness was completely blotted out.
She decided that Richard was at last being friendly
with his neighbours, that he was beginning to see that the
aloof and distant attitude he had adopted towards them
for the past year was not quite the thing these days. Yes,
that was the explanation, decided Vicky ... but as the
evening wore on and she basked in the sunshine of Richard's smiles and attentiveness, the explanation did not
satisfy her at all.

CHAPTER THREE

THEY had been married for just over a fortnight and Vicky, her new life obviously suiting her, had already blossomed into a girl of such beauty that even her father remarked on it.

'I always thought there could be no improvement,' he told her in his gruff Lancashire voice. 'But, my love, marriage has made a rare beauty of you. It obviously agrees with you.'

She laughed, a happy girlish laugh.

'You were so right, Father, when you said a woman doesn't reach the peak of happiness until she's married. Oh, but I'm so very much in love!—and so deliriously happy that I sometimes become afraid it can't last.'

'Tell me, child, how long have you been in love with Richard?'

'You guessed?'

'My dear, you and I have been so close that we're both able to read one another's minds. Yes, of course I guessed.'

'I'll bet you didn't guess when it all began?' she challenged roguishly.

'Don't tell me it was love at first sight?'

'Truly.' But she paused a moment. 'Well, almost,' she amended.

'Just like your mother! Well, who'd have thought it!'

'I never dreamed he'd ever love me. You see, there was the girl he used to go about with, Louisa Austin.'

For some strange reason her father avoided her eyes as he said,

'She was unimportant in his life. A mere flirtation, my pet. You mustn't ever worry that pretty head of yours that Richard will ever bother with her again.'

Vicky's smile faded; she could not have explained why a tiny cloud had appeared on her sunny horizon. There had been a note of grimness in her father's voice as he spoke the last sentence. She had heard it before, but only when some threat was made to one of his carefully planned schemes.

'I must be off,' she declared, looking at the clock. 'Richard hates me to be a second late for meals.'

'The stern husband, is he?'

She laughed, her vista cloudless again.

'He is ... but I like it!'

It was her father's turn to laugh.

'So long as you like it then it's all right. But don't allow him to become too masterful, pet. You're not to let yourself be domineered—besides, anyone who treats you wrongly will have me to deal with!'

Again Vicky lost a little of her buoyancy. Her father had asserted that he and she could read one another's minds, but there had been numerous times recently when she had not only been unable to read his mind, but had been totally baffled by both his manner and his cryptic way of speaking.

'I can't conceive of Richard's treating me any differently from what he treats me now. He's so in love, and I still wonder at his choosing me, out of all the lovely, wealthy society girls he could obviously have had had he wished.'

Again her father's expression was hidden from her as he said,

'I always told you, love, that you were a gracious lady,

as good as any in the land. Richard saw this, and fell in love with you. And now you're settled for life in a lovely stately home and with a husband who's *somebody*.'

'It turned out just as you wanted it to, didn't it?'

'Yes, my love, it did.'

'And after all your scheming, your search for ways in which I could meet people like Richard, it happened quite naturally in the end—without your scheming!' She couldn't help that, but softened it with a hug and a kiss. 'I really must be off,' she said. 'We're to see you about seven this evening?'

'Yes. Vicky ...'

She drew away, puzzled by his tone.

'Yes?'

'If you and Richard want to be on your own ... I mean, I don't want to intrude. I'm only a rough sort of bloke and might not seem to fit in at the Manor——' He got no further. Vicky, adopting a severity of expression that was totally new to her father, told him in no uncertain terms that as *her father* he would always fit in at the Manor.

'Richard thinks a lot of you,' she added. 'He always speaks highly of your business acumen—in fact, he says the other day that he wished he possessed the same gift for making money.'

'He did?' Wallace appeared to be gratified by this.

'Yes, but I don't really know why he should want to make money; he has all that anyone could need.'

Wallace said nothing and a moment later he was accompanying his daughter as she crossed the lawn fronting the bungalow, at the end of which was a small gate leading to the more natural part of the grounds and then to the foot of the low hill over which the Manor was situated.

'I'm so glad you're not too far away,' he said.

'I wouldn't have gone too far away.'

'You'd have gone where your husband wanted you to go.'

'I'd not have left you, Father. As things are I can see you every day if I want, and you can come regularly to our home. It's a perfect arrangement in every single way.'

'So it is, my precious.' He kissed her cheek, stood at the gate until she was out of sight, then turned back on to the lawn and walked briskly towards the house.

It was five minutes to one when Vicky arrived home; Richard was in the hall and his eyes slid to the clock.

'I'll just wash my face and hands and be down in two minutes,' she promised, giving him a smile of glancing tenderness. 'Father's fine and we had a nice little chat in the garden. Isn't the weather lovely!'

'Very good indeed, but it *is* early summer, so we should be having good weather.'

Vicky went up on tiptoe and kissed him on the lips. She expected his hands to come to her waist and span it, as they so often did, but this time they remained at his sides and, after an uncertain glance at his expressionless face she ran from him, to mount the curving balustraded staircase. Her bedroom, with its connecting door to her husband's room, was known as the Blue Room on account of the walls being covered with a delicate shade of blue silk, embossed with flowers, trees and birds. The coved ceiling was painted to represent a night sky, with numerous stars against a background of blue. At first Vicky was not sure whether or not she liked it; her bedroom at the bungalow had been so light in comparison. However, her husband said it would 'grow on her', and this had proved to be true. In only a fortnight she had come to love her room ... especially as her husband came to her every night, sharing the great tester bed which was hung with dainty blue drapes of silk lace.

She was a little longer than she expected, having decided to change her dress, putting on a light apple-green
sun-dress with a flared skirt and straps for the bodice
support.

'How do I look?' she asked as she came down the
stairs again. Richard was still there, having just replaced
the telephone receiver on its rest. His face was taut, and
two little grey lines had appeared at the sides of his
mouth. 'Is anything wrong?' Vicky forgot her first question as anxiety darkened her eyes. 'Bad news or something?' Her glance slid quite naturally to the telephone.

He shook his head.

'No—nothing you would understand, Vicky.'

She put her hand in his, felt his fingers curl in a way
that had become familiar, and she turned her head to
slant him a tender look.

'I shall be going out after lunch,' he told her when
they were half way through the meal. 'So we shall have to
cancel our trip into town, I'm afraid.'

'Oh ...' A wave of disappointment flooded over her.
'Can't I come with you?'

'No, darling, I'm afraid not.'

'Is it business?' she asked, thinking of the telephone
call.

He made no answer for a moment and then,

'Not entirely, dear. It's a private matter, though, so
I must go alone.'

She looked at his face across the table and wondered
if it were her imagination or whether he really did look
rather drawn and haggard. Vicky's concern increased, but
she was prudent enough to see that her husband was in no
mood for answering questions. Her appetite had gone and
she put down her knife and fork. Richard, frowning at
the action, told her almost abruptly to eat her lunch.

'I'm not hungry any more,' she said without thinking.

'Any more? You mean that you were hungry but now you're not?'

She nodded dumbly, hurt by his tone.

He ate in silence after that, absorbed in his own thoughts—which were definitely not happy ones, decided Vicky, her concern for him increasing all the time. What was wrong? If only he would tell her then she might be able to comfort him in some way. Glancing up at length, he told her again to eat her lunch.

'I don't——'

'Eat it,' he said, and she obeyed, though every mouthful seemed to choke her. She was relieved when at last the meal was finished. Richard wasted no time in getting away and as she watched the car slide smoothly from the forecourt she felt so depressed that she could have cried.

She went out to the garden, found a seat beneath the trees and sat there, thinking about the events leading up to her marriage ... the events and the swiftness with which they had progressed to that wonderful day when, clad in white, and with the two little granddaughters of Mrs Basset—a very old friend of Wallace—as her bridesmaids, Vicky had become the wife of Richard Sherrand.

She recalled the day when Richard had shown her round his home. He had asked her many times if she liked this or that, if she would change anything had she the chance. He had told her a little about himself; she had read much between the lines and realised that he and his stepmother were sworn enemies. She still drew an allowance from the estate. She was an incurable alcoholic and gambler, but managed to live in a large house and keep three servants. All this came from the Whitethorn estate, and although Richard had skipped much regarding his stepmother Vicky realised that the drain on Richard's income must be almost crippling. It seemed, from what

Vicky had gathered from something her father had said, that this stepmother, if she wished, could by law claim a great deal more than she was doing. But when Vicky tried to draw her father out a little more he shut up like a clam and Vicky gave up, deciding that it was not her business anyway. But she did wonder how her father knew so much about Richard's private affairs.

After the visit that afternoon Vicky was a constant companion of Richard, who showed quite plainly that he was more than a little interested in her. He came often to the bungalow and in turn Vicky and her father were regular visitors to Whitethorn Manor. Then, one evening after they had dined, Richard asked Wallace if he and Vicky would like to walk in the gardens, as it was such a balmy evening. Wallace declined but urged Vicky to take the stroll with Richard.

'You might have had some inkling,' she said to her father afterwards. For Richard had kissed her that night and immediately asked her to marry him. She recalled how calm he had been, how unemotional. Yet he had taken her into his arms when, shyly, she had said yes, she would marry him, and he had kissed her with a sort of reverence, but there had been no passion in his manner with her. She had admired him for his control, which lasted until the night of their wedding when, coming in to her and seeing her standing there, in a filmy night-gown that revealed every line and curve of her soft young body, he had taken her to him with an ardour that had swept her to heights of ecstasy she had never dreamed existed. And so it had been since, but now ... For the first time Richard had spoken sharply to her, and he had gone off without her after promising to take her into Sheffield to do some shopping.

However, Vicky soon put her disappointment behind her and saw the situation from her husband's angle. He had private business to attend to, so he did not want her with him. There was nothing to become upset about, she told herself, and straightway threw off that little tinge of dejection which still remained.

She called to Kaliph, Richard's Labrador with whom she had immediately made friends on the afternoon when Richard had shown her over the house. And each morning she was now greeted by the dog as soon as she came from her bedroom.

'We're going for a long walk,' she told him, 'so I hope you're prepared.'

She strode through the gardens to the woodlands, then out on to the tree-lined road leading to the village. All around were the moorlands, wild and mysterious when shrouded in mist, as they often were, but tranquil and attractive when basking in the sunshine, as they were to-day. In the valley the stream danced merrily over the stones and moss then dropped down to form a beautiful cascade over an abrupt shelving of rock which, having been harder than the rocks surrounding it, had resisted the stream's destruction, but which would sooner or later succumb and then the river's bed would smooth out. To Vicky's right were several quarries, disused now and overgrown with ferns and foxgloves, with tall grasses and climbing plants, and even with colourful rhododendrons and the like. The quarries were picturesque in their soft clothing of greenery, but at one time they had been harsh blots on the lovely Derbyshire landscape.

Vicky whistled to the dog, who had strayed on to the moors in search of anything that moved. He came bounding towards her and she kept him at her side, a little anxious in case of cars or other vehicles coming along the road. One did come eventually, and the driver stopped.

'Want a lift?' he inquired, winding down the window.

'No, thank you, I'm out for a walk.'

'You've a long way to go.' The young man was laughing, but his eyes were taking in the most attractive picture of Vicky standing there, her hair teased by the breeze, her gay sun-dress clinging to her figure as the breeze played tricks with this too. The dog decided to bark, as if warning the motorist that he would guard his mistress with his life.

'How do you know I've a long way to go?' Vicky could not resist asking.

'Because you're miles from anywhere.'

'I like walking. This is no distance at all.'

'Why, where do you live?'

She paused before answering, fully aware that it was not the thing to be talking to a stranger like this, and on such a lonely stretch of road. But he was nice, she decided, examining his slightly freckled face, his full generous mouth, his light blue eyes and fair hair swept back from a clear wide forehead.

'I live at Whitethorn Manor,' she told him at length.

He gave a start and for a while there was silence between them. Vicky, faintly puzzled by the man's attitude, would have moved on, but she was stopped by his voice saying,

'Whitethorn Manor, eh? I just happen to be going there.'

Vicky blinked at him.

'You are? What for?'

Again there was silence.

'Who are you?' he said eventually, eyeing her up and down again.

She coloured, a tinge of anger rising because of his question and because of the rather businesslike expression that had erased the laughter from his eyes.

'What's that to you? If you'll excuse me I'll be on my way.'

'Hi, wait a minute,' he called as she strode away from the car. 'I'm sorry if I seemed rude ...' Vicky carried on; the car soon drew up alongside her again and she stopped. The dog gave another bark, but it was not the threatening kind; vaguely it registered with Vicky that Kaliph had not taken a dislike to the driver of the car. 'I'm to see a Mr Sherrand up at Whitethorn Manor. He'll be in, I suppose?'

Automatically she shook her head.

'No, he isn't. He went out after lunch and won't be back for some time.'

The young man frowned and looked down at a folder which lay on the passenger seat of the car.

'A wasted journey,' he muttered to himself. And, in a louder voice, 'I've an appointment with him for three o'clock. I've come all the way from Manchester.'

'It's a quarter to three now.'

'I know. I had my timing correct.' He paused, looking vexed. 'I don't suppose you can help me?'

Vicky shook her head.

'No, I don't know anything about your visit. My husband didn't mention that he had an appointment this afternoon. In fact, if he hadn't gone out on his own we'd both have gone into Sheffield, so you wouldn't have found him in. Are you sure you have the day right?' she added, looking at the folder.

'Your husband ...' The young man seemed not to have heard anything else of what Vicky had said. 'You're Mr Sherrand's wife?' His tone had become distinctly respectful, but his expression was one of disbelief. 'You don't look old enough to be married—if you'll forgive my saying so.'

She laughed, noting that his face relaxed as she did so.

'I'm not very old,' she said. 'About this appointment —I feel worried that you've wasted your time. If I could help I would, but as I've said, I know nothing about your visit.'

For a long moment the young man seemed undecided, then, as if on impulse, he said,

'I think that perhaps you can help me. I've been sent out by my firm to survey some land your husband's selling. I have the map here showing the area and location of the land, but of course I can't just go roaming all over a person's land when he isn't there—or at least, without the authority of someone able to give it. Would you come back with me and take me around?'

'My husband has land for sale?' Vicky shook her head. 'I think you must be mistaken.' Yet he had sold land to her father, she thought. *Was* he in financial difficulties, as her father had suggested? It would seem like it, for otherwise he wouldn't be thinking of selling land which had formed part of the estate for hundreds of years.

'I have all the particulars here.' He tapped the file as he spoke. 'You didn't know he was selling his land?'

'No, I didn't, but it must be right, of course, as you have all the particulars relating to it.' Vicky paused in indecision. The man had come a long way and it seemed quite unnecessary to send him away without doing what he had been sent to do. Besides, Richard would obviously be glad that his wife had used her common sense and let the man take a look at the land. But she did ask again whether he had the date right.

'Yes, I can show it to you.' He made to open the file, but Vicky said no, it did not matter. 'Will you come with me, then?'

She still hesitated, and the man did then insist on opening the file. She was shown the instructions which the man had from his employers, a firm of builders whose name Vicky already knew, and she gave a little gasp. This particular firm had been her father's competitor for years, and many were the times when they had put in a tender which had undercut that of Wallace with the result that he had lost the work.

'They can't be making any profit to speak of!' he had often said angrily. 'I never aim for high returns, so I know my figure's reasonable. They're determined to put me out of business but, by heaven, they'll not do it while I've breath in my body!'

And now Richard was considering selling land to this company.

She got into the car after putting Kaliph in the back, the young man saying he did not mind at all. It was the firm's car in any case.

'This land,' she said once they were on their way, 'what is your firm going to do with it?'

'Build an estate, providing they can get planning permission, which they're fairly confident of doing.'

'An estate?' she gasped. 'What kind of an estate?'

'A housing estate. You don't take to the idea, evidently.'

She said nothing; her mind was in chaos. Something was surely wrong, for Richard would never sell land for the building of a housing estate. Why, there would then be shops and offices, roads and schools and works—

'How much land is my husband selling?' she asked abruptly.

'At first, four hundred acres, but we can have more later if we want it, which I believe we shall—Here, take a look at the plan of the land which is for sale.' Reaching to the shelf under the dash, he brought out the file which he had removed when Vicky entered the car. 'You do understand maps?'

'Yes,' she answered, not without a little hint of tartness. 'My father's a builder.'

'He is? What's the name of his firm?'

'I'd rather not say,' she returned, and at the curt finality of her voice the young man lapsed into silence which lasted until they reached the Manor and alighted from the car. Kaliph bounded off to the back courtyard where he knew he could get a drink; Vicky invited the man into the house, asking him to open up the map fully so that she could see the extent of the land being offered for sale. This he did, after telling her his name.

'I'm John Bailey—I should have introduced myself before. Sorry about that. You're Mrs Richard Sherrand, of course?'

Vicky merely nodded, wondering if she should go over to the bungalow and fetch her father. He would be busy, though, in his office. Besides, to go over and fetch him would waste time and, for some reason she could not explain, Vicky wanted to learn more about this land deal before her husband's return.

'This is the land?' she was saying a few moments later when John Bailey, having opened out the map on a large table in the hall, indicated a ringed area on the eastern side of the Manor. Vicky caught her breath.

'This takes in land on the other side of the hill,' she said in choking accents. 'A great area of land.'

'Yes, that's right. It won't interfere with the view from the Manor—If you look at the contours you'll see this. On the other side of the hill there's only a bungalow——' He stopped to point this out. 'They'll eventually be surrounded by property, but that's the luck of the draw, isn't it? No one's view is safe these days, not with building going on all over the place.'

'They don't usually build on estates like this.'

'Oh, I wouldn't say that! It's the so-called rich who are being forced to sell their land—Oh, lord! I'm awfully sorry, Mrs Sherrand. What an unthinking fool I am—and you not knowing that your husband's selling anyway. Please forgive me; I do apologise.' He stared at her anxiously, at a face that was a mask, stiff and cold, like the rest of her body.

'You want to go over and look at this land?' she said at last, and the man nodded eagerly.

'I've got to survey it, and form an opinion as to whether its purchase for building would be a viable proposition or not.'

They went in silence, John Bailey suddenly grasping the fact that the lady by his side was exceedingly upset, to say the least. He told her where the borders were, but she examined the map for herself. Yes, the bungalow would be somewhere in the middle of this proposed housing estate.

'That's the bungalow—but of course you must know it.' He pointed for all that. 'A beautiful place judging by what we can see from here. Must be a wealthy man who's built it. You know him, Mrs Sherrand?'

'Yes, I do know him.' Her voice was not like her own, she thought. It was choked and stiff and it was with difficulty that she spoke at all. 'Four hundred acres, you said?'

'Correct.' He wandered away from her, gazing around then referring to his map again. 'I'd like to take some soil samples if I may. One never knows, buyers of properties might want to start things like nurseries. I daresay a few acres of glass would pay off here. Tomato growing and other pricey commodities ...' He trailed off, noticing how pale she was. 'I'm sorry ... you don't care for the ideas of rows and rows of greenhouses? It *is* over the

hill, you know, Mrs Sherrand, so you won't have your
view spoiled, as I said.' He seemed concerned about her,
but at the same time he obviously had an eye for business.
'It'll take me some time to do what I've come for, so if
you'd rather leave me ...?'

'Yes, I would.' And without another word she wheeled
away and went back to the Manor.

How could Richard sell land which would ruin her
father's view?—not only that, but the value of the bungalow would drop tremendously. It would not be worth half
what it had cost.

It was over an hour before John Bailey returned.
Vicky, giving him no encouragement to stay, merely
offered him a cup of tea, but at the same time told him
that she had not much time to spare.

'You must get in touch with my husband,' she added.
'I'll tell him you've called, of course, and that you have
done your surveying.'

'Thank you. Er—I'm very sorry——'

'It's not your fault, Mr Bailey. And now, I'm afraid
you must excuse me ...'

She stood by the window and watched his car draw
away, then speed smoothly along the tree-lined drive to
the bend where he was soon hidden from view. She closed
her eyes, wondering how she was to tell her father the
dreadful news. Richard must be in dire straits to sell
his land in such quantities. But if he did have to sell
surely he could have sold from another part of the estate,
not close to, and surrounding, the bungalow.

She waited with growing impatience for his return. Yet
when she eventually did see the car coming along the
drive she felt all she wanted to do was run away. However, she remained where she was, forcing a smile to her
lips as Richard came into the drawing-room and, re-

turning her smile, kissed her lightly on the lips.

'A man's been here,' she told him without preamble, 'by the name of John Bailey. He was from a firm of builders called——'

'John Bailey! He's been here?' Anger brought the colour creeping along Richard's mouth. 'What right— What was he doing?'

'Surveying the land you have to sell, Richard. It's— it's for a housing estate, he told me, and it'll take every bit of land surrounding my father's land.'

Richard, looking down into her white face, suddenly forgot his anger in his concern for her. He held out his arms and she ran into them, resting her head against his breast.

'My darling,' he said softly, 'your fears are groundless. I did intend selling some land, but I've changed my mind. This estate remains intact.'

'Changed your mind?' she said, drawing away from him. 'Oh, Richard, do you mean it?'

'I certainly do, my dear. How unpleasant that man's visit must have been for you. I don't know what went wrong, but I cancelled his visit more than a month ago. The inefficiency of some of these firms appals me. They've obviously lost the letter I sent—or rather, that my lawyer sent.' He felt her body sag in his arms, sag with relief, but the strain had told on her and in spite of her efforts to restrain them, the tears came to her eyes. 'Hush, my love, you mustn't cry. It's all for nothing. Your father's bungalow is quite safe.'

'But you were originally intending to sell the land?'

'Yes,' he said with a sigh, 'I was, Vicky.'

'And you would have sold that particular land—surrounding our bungalow?'

He seemed pained, but only for a moment or two.

'At the time I first contemplated selling, my love, I hadn't come to know your father properly, and I hadn't even met you.'

'I see.' Relief swept over her as she thought about this. 'I suppose it takes some time for a deal like that to be put into operation. Father used to become so annoyed at delays in obtaining land.'

Her husband nodded his head.

'I began negotiations with the building firm not very long after you and your father moved into the bungalow.'

'You must have been—short of money.' Vicky spoke hesitantly, fearing her husband might be vexed at the idea of her speaking about his private affairs. But to her surprise he actually smiled down at her and said yes, he was in difficulties at that time.

'However,' he went on, drawing her close to his heart again, 'it's all over now. I managed to—to put things right.'

She looked up, only vaguely conscious of the slight hesitation he had made. She was too happy to think of anything but the fact that John Bailey's visit was all a mistake, that the land was not being sold and therefore her father's bungalow was safe. She snuggled more closely into her husband's arms, and they stood for a long while, both silent, both deep in thought.

'Did you manage to do the business you went out to do?' she asked at last, raising her head to look into his face.

'I did.' Abrupt his voice, and his arms about her seemed to have stiffened. 'It wasn't exactly business, as I mentioned.'

Vicky said nothing; she was faintly uneasy without knowing why this should be. Her husband, suddenly appearing to sense this uneasiness, bent his head and kissed her tenderly on the lips.

'I love you,' she whispered, almost before he had drawn his lips away. 'How has it come about that I'm so very very lucky?'

To her surprise he seemed to wince.

'It's I who am lucky, my dearest.' His eyes were brooding, though, and he appeared to have something profoundly troublesome on his mind. 'Yes, indeed, it's I who am lucky.' He held her close; she felt his long lithe body quiver as if at the nearness of hers. 'What a darling you are! Sweet, unsophisticated, loving ... what else could any man want in a wife?'

She laughed a little shakily, and said he would surely spoil her with such flattery.

'You're as bad as my father,' she told him.

'He adores you. I wish I'd had a little affection from my father.'

'I'm sorry for anyone who hasn't a father like mine.'

'And I for anyone who hasn't a wife like mine,' returned Richard gallantly and, encircling her in his arms again, he held her close, protectively, so that all her fears were dissolved in the knowledge that her husband loved her and always would love her.

CHAPTER FOUR

SEVERAL idyllic days sped by, with Vicky spending her time in rearranging some of the furniture, after asking her husband's permission and then discussing the changes with him. She had certainly a wonderful flair for interior design, Richard was soon admitting, and went on to say that whatever she did was bound to be an improvement.

'You must get Snowy to help you,' he told her one day when, coming in unexpectedly, he found her trying to move a heavy secretairs of black lacquer decorated with gold on the doors and pediment. 'Don't let me find you struggling like this again.' His voice was stern, his eyes glinting with anger. She knew at once that he was thinking that a wife of his ought not to be engaged in so menial a task as moving furniture without help from one or more of the servants. In fact, she was to supervise, that was all, he said.

'I'm sorry.' She straightened up, her face flushed, her dress not nearly as immaculate as usual. His grey eyes slid over her, but he made no comment on her appearance, a fact for which she was exceedingly relieved. 'Is Snowy at liberty? He was mending an electrical iron for Lucy when I last saw him.'

'So you were in the kitchen?'

She nodded.

'At home I liked being in the kitchen, seeing to the meals—I don't mean cooking them,' she hastened to add. 'Grace, our cook, wouldn't even have allowed me to do any of the important cooking.'

'You shouldn't be in the kitchen, Vicky,' said Richard, though not unkindly. 'Surely you can find some more pleasant place to spend your time?'

'I shall probably help you,' she said, laughing.

'Me? In what way?'

'You have accounts appertaining to the estate. I often did Father's accounts for him. He was so tired at night when he came home that sometimes he'd just flop into a chair and fall asleep ...' Vicky let her voice fade as she noticed the change in her husband's expression. 'Is anything wrong?'

'I was just trying to imagine Wallace as you describe him, coming home dead beat and dropping off to sleep. He'd be off again the next morning, working hard again.' He stopped, his face reflective. 'To think that he's worked so hard for his money and now ...' A deep sigh, and a quivering of his mouth. Vicky went to him and, tucking her arm in his, looked up into his dark face and said,

'Sometimes, Richard, you're so puzzling to me. You're as bad as Father when you use such unfathomable expressions.'

'Your father? What unfathomable expressions does he use?'

'I can't remember specific ones.' Vicky wrinkled her nose as she tried to concentrate. 'It was before we were married mostly. He said strange things which I couldn't understand. I still wonder what made him send you that first invitation. I thought he was thinking he might do some sort of business deal with you, but that wasn't the reason obviously, because you haven't done a business deal together, have you?' To her amazement he turned from her abruptly, making no answer but changing the subject, telling her once again that she must not move anything heavy. She looked at her hand, which a few seconds ago had been tucked into his. Her mouth quivered; she wanted to go to him, to lift her lips in an offering of her love. But Richard seemed so far away ... so very far away.

'I won't do any more for the present,' she said in a flat little voice. 'Do you mind if I go over and see Father?'

He turned, his eyes inquiring.

'Have I ever minded, Vicky?'

'No, but I might stay for lunch.'

'Why?' he asked briefly.

'I don't really know why I want to stay for lunch. Maybe I feel the need for com——' She broke off, staggered that she could have been going to say a thing like that.

'Comfort?' Richard's voice was sharp yet anxious. 'Vicky, what on earth do you mean?'

She shook her head, impatient with herself.

'It was silly—a slip of the tongue.'

'You ought not to be in need of comfort, my dear.'

'No——' A shaky laugh escaped her. 'I can't explain, Richard, so please don't ask me.' She thought of these past few days, and the sheer bliss that each one had brought her. Richard had worked during the mornings in his study, while Vicky had wandered over to see her father for a short while. On her return she had occupied herself in the pleasurable task of making certain alterations in some of the rooms, taking out items of furniture which she considered inconsistent with the general layout and putting other items in their place. At lunch she would be with her husband and afterwards they would either go out in the car or wander, hand in hand, over the moorlands and valleys. Dinner later, in the warm romantic setting of candlelight and flowers, then perhaps another stroll, shorter this time, in the garden, then to their rooms. Vicky would wait, her heart throbbing wildly, for the central door to swing inwards, and her husband would be there, smiling tenderly, his arms wide and inviting. Yes, there had been nothing to mar the happiness, yet now, for some obscure reason, Vicky knew a return of that uneasiness she had experienced on a couple of previous occasions.

'You can't explain?' Richard's voice repeating her words broke into her reflections. 'You've just accused *me* of being cryptic,' he reminded her with a dry inflection.

'I know—but it's different,' she said lamely. 'As I said, I can't explain.'

'You must be able to explain why you have this need to run to your father for comfort, Vicky.'

'Take no notice. I don't know myself why I said it.'

He was not satisfied, but made no further attempt to extract an explanation from her.

'Are you staying at the bungalow for lunch, then?' he wanted to know.

'I——' She paused, undecided. 'I love having lunch with you, Richard.' Her voice had dropped to a whisper and so the plea in it was missed by her husband.

'And I enjoy having mine with you, Vicky. However, if you really want a change, then by all means go to your father——'

'I don't want a change,' she protested, her eyes misting up, dimming her vision. 'You and I always have lunch together.'

'Then what is this all about?' Gently he took her by the shoulders, drawing her to him. 'We shall have our lunch together, my darling, just as we're used to doing.'

Vicky managed a smile, her world bright and sunny again.

'I'm very silly,' she owned deprecatingly. 'I imagine things.'

'I'm in complete agreement with you,' her husband returned with a hint of amusement, 'and for that reason I shan't insist on knowing what those things are that you imagine.'

'Because they're unimportant?'

'Precisely.'

She looked up at him, her lips quivering tremulously. Richard, his attention fixed, seemed for a long while to be taking in all he saw, taking it in deeply, absorbing it just as if it were something entirely new that was there before his eyes. She blinked, shy and tensed, her whole being effected by his nearness, by the touch of his hands, by the expression on his face when, bending slowly, he pressed his lips to her in a kiss of mastery and possession.

'How very lovely you are, Vicky.'

A long while later she was thinking of those words while she sat before her dressing-table, brushing her hair. It was wonderful to know that the beauty of which her father so often spoke was giving her husband so much pleasure. For the first time Vicky was examining herself with intense interest—noticing her eyes with their long curling lashes, her 'turned-up' nose, as her father so often referred to it—mostly when he was reminiscing about her mother. She looked at her mouth, which Richard obviously loved to kiss. And a smile broke. Life was good!

Not that it had been anything else for Vicky, but as her father had so wisely maintained, a woman does not reach the peak of happiness until she is married to the man she loves, and who loves her. It was providential, she mused, that she should marry a man of aristocratic birth, since this was her father's dream, his final ambition in life. Yet it had happened naturally, and not aided by his scheming at all, just as she had laughingly reminded him a few days ago. Now his dream had materialised he was content, appearing to have settled down to a tranquil, uncomplicated existence which must seem like heaven after the zealous activity of the past forty years or so. Had his dream not come to fruition, then undoubtedly he would have persevered until it did, simply because he never allowed anything to beat him, just as he had so vehemently declared so many times.

Glancing at the clock, Vicky noticed that it was almost half past seven, and as Richard liked to have an aperitif in the drawing-room before dinner she hastened to get dressed, putting on a long gown of flowered black nylon, full-skirted and with the unusual feature of having a white insert to the bodice which was split down the front and then laced with black silk cord. The high neckline was frilled, as were the cuffs and the hem of the skirt. The underslip was full, being made up of several layers of white nylon, and the result was that the skirt of the dress flowed out, swaying as Vicky walked.

She came down the wide staircase to see her husband going to the telephone at the far end of the hall. What an arresting figure he made! So tall and straight and slim. So many times she had told herself she was lucky to have such a superlative man for a husband, and she was telling herself again as, stopping before she reached the last stair, she watched him pick up the receiver and dial a number. It occurred to her that she ought to make her presence known, since Richard, with his back to her, had no idea that she was there. The thought of revealing herself was vague, though, Vicky's entire interest being with her husband. Absurdly she felt she would be quite content to remain here, just looking at his back for half an hour or more.

He was speaking; she listened without fully realising she was doing so.

'... your letter this morning. I'd prefer you to refrain from this direct communication and leave everything to the solicitors.' Richard's voice was brittle, and frigidly austere. 'Yes,' he was saying, obviously in answer to a brief question just put to him, 'you are entitled to half this——' His voice was cut, obviously by an interruption on the other end of the line. 'I have to accept it—I *have* accepted it, but these things take time. It's quite impossible for me to satisfy your——' Again there seemed to be an interruption and this time Vicky noticed the dark and angry frown that settled on her husband's forehead. He was listening; the frown gradually deepened to a scowl of sheer hatred. At last he himself broke in to say that he would no longer tolerate 'these letters of abuse!'

The telephone receiver was about to be replaced and Vicky, guiltily aware that she should not have remained there, listening to something that had nothing to do with her, stepped back swiftly, managing to negotiate several stairs before coming to a stop as Richard turned. She then continued down the stairs—slowly, as if to impress on him that this had been her speed all the time—a smile fluttering to her lips.

She saw no answering smile but instead a stern and questioning look upon her husband's face.

'How long have you been there?' he demanded almost harshly.

'Not—not l-long. Why do you ask?'

He was standing at the foot of the stairs, looking up at her, and for a fleeting moment his thoughts were diverted as he allowed his eyes to wander over her lovely figure before coming to rest on her face. She was flustered, aware that she had eavesdropped, and fearing her husband knew she had. How angry he would be! And surely he would despise her!

'Did you hear any part of what I was saying?' The keen grey eyes seemed to be probing far beneath the negative expression she had forced herself to assume.

Almost without knowing it Vicky was shaking her

head, and it was with a sort of wondering disbelief that she heard herself say,

'No, Richard, I didn't hear anything. I've only just come down ...' and she began to descend the final few stairs until she reached the last one. 'Do you like my dress?' She took hold of the sides and pulled them out. Richard, plainly relieved, held out his hand for her to slip hers into it, which she did, her heartbeats returning to normal after the racing which had been induced by fear.

They dined cosily and intimately, by the light of many candles. Vicky kept up a bright front, chatting happily to her husband, but it was inevitable that his words over the telephone should keep coming back to her, and in consequence several questions darted about in her mind. To whom had Richard been speaking? He had certainly been furiously angry—but no wonder, if he had been receiving letters of abuse! Vicky could not imagine anyone having the temerity to write letters of abuse to a man like Richard. Was someone threatening him? It had seemed like it, yet *who* would want to threaten him? she wondered.

'Vicky, what are you thinking about?' Richard's voice, low and cultured, reached her across the table, breaking her reverie. She met his keen grey eyes and wondered what lay behind their apparently amused expression. 'You're not with me, my darling, and that doesn't suit me at all.'

'I'm sorry. Nothing important,' she hastened to add, just in case he should begin a series of questions that might cause her to make a slip and reveal the fact that she had overheard some of what he had been saying. 'Isn't this steak delicious? You know, Richard, until I tasted your cook's meals I'd have argued that our cook was the best in the country.'

He seemed gratified by her praise of the cook.

'I won't take credit for her being here, though,' he said. 'My father found her—or rather, stole her from one of his best friends. He offered to double her wages and this she couldn't resist, so she came to us.'

'That wasn't very fair of your father——' Vicky stopped. Then apologised.

'You've no need to,' laughed Richard. 'Everyone deplored my father's action. Needless to say, it was the end of the friendship.'

After a silent moment Vicky said, a little hesitantly,

'Your father ... you haven't spoken about him very much at all.'

'You'd like to know more about him?' Suddenly the full mouth was thin, just as Vicky had seen it on the day she had first spoken to Richard, and now, as then, she sensed that he was either recalling an unpleasant memory, or regretting something. 'We didn't have anything in common, so there's not much to tell you. I left home when he married my stepmother, as you already know.'

'That was a shame. After all, it was *your* home.'

'Yes, I missed it very much.' His expression was brooding as he added, 'I often used to wonder if I would ever come back at all.'

'Oh, but you were bound to! As soon as your father died you would be the owner.' Vicky was cutting her steak and missed the harsh twist of her husband's lips.

'Yes,' he murmured expressionlessly. 'I would be the owner.'

'It's said that your stepmother was extravagant.' Vicky looked uncertainly at him. 'Ought I not to talk about such things, Richard?'

'They're unprofitable, my dear. However, you are my wife and it's only natural that you should be interested in my background.'

'Yes. You see,' she went on naïvely, 'you know everything about my background, don't you?'

'I believe so—unless you have a skeleton in the cupboard,' he added teasingly.

'We haven't anything to be ashamed of. My father's never committed a dishonest act, in spite of his being a keen businessman. And I——' Vicky spread her hands and laughed with her eyes. 'I can't recollect having done anything more reprehensible than punching a girl on the nose.'

'You ... what?' Richard's eyes opened wide. 'Really?'

'She spoke disparagingly about my father. I went to an expensive school, as you know, and the girls there were all daughters of the—er—people like you.' She looked apologetically at him, a circumstance that seemed to afford him considerable amusement. 'Well, she talked about my father being a common bricklayer—he was, at first, but then he had his own business. I couldn't stand by and listen to that, could I?'

'Indeed, no,' agreed her husband, lips twitching.

'So I gave her a punch on the nose, and made it bleed.' Vicky glanced down to her plate and picked up a choice piece of steak to pop into her mouth. 'By the way,' she went on when Richard made no comment, 'please don't mention this to Father. He would be quite shocked if he knew I'd acted in such an unladylike fashion. He'd actually feel he'd failed in some way.'

'Yes,' musingly, 'I can imagine he would. A perfectionist with high ideals and even higher ambitions.'

'Yes, you've read him perfectly.'

'I'd better beware,' he said presently, veering the subject a little. 'I can see I must take care.'

'Take care?'

'Not to upset you in any way. I might find myself with a black eye!'

She looked up and laughed at him across the table. And as he watched her in the glow from the candles, a strange expression crossed his face. But then his mouth moved convulsively, and his grey eyes shadowed so that Vicky's smile faded as a feeling of anxiety erased the lightness of spirit she had just revealed by her gay laughter.

'I could never hurt you, Richard.' The words came slowly, the automatic answer to what he had said. She added immediately, 'Is anything wrong, Richard?'

'Wrong, dear?'

'You looked—sad ...'

'I'm not sad, darling,' he hastened to reassure her, his face clearing on the instant. 'What made you say a thing like that?'

She shook her head vaguely. She had a strong suspicion that Richard was deceiving her, that he really was sad over something. She bit her lip, realising—not for the first time—that there was something missing as regards the intimacy which should have existed between her husband and herself. It was not *complete*. She supposed this must be owing to her own sensitivity regarding the difference in her background and Richard's. She had, from the first, been keenly aware of this difference and had in consequence considered herself inferior to her husband. She knew now that unless she could discard this inferiority complex she and Richard would never come as close as she wished them to do. If they had been close at this time then she could have insisted that he tell her what was troubling him; as things were, she felt she had not the right to do so.

'I don't know why I said it,' she lied when, glancing at her husband, she saw that he was waiting patiently for her to answer him. 'It was just that you looked—different.'

'I'm sorry, my love. I assure you I'm very happy and have nothing on my mind.' He looked down at his plate as he spoke and although Vicky kept her eyes on him he did not glance up for some time. When he did he was plainly amused about something.

'Tell me more about this girl you decided to beat up. You weren't expelled, obviously, but you must have been punished for your behaviour?'

'She didn't report it. She knew she'd done wrong herself by saying those things about my father.'

'So you got away with it?'

'Yes, thank goodness. I hate to think what my father would have said if I'd had that on my report at the end of term.'

'He was strict with you at times, then?'

'Yes, very strict. He was afraid, you see, that I'd be spoiled.'

Her husband smiled at this and said softly,

'He needn't have feared; you're not the girl to become spoiled.' There was a certain tenderness in his voice that immediately brought back her lightness of spirit.

'Thank you,' she returned demurely. And then, 'I take after my mother, so I'm very lucky indeed.'

'Your father speaks about your mother a great deal?'

'Not a great deal, but I'm sure she's never long out of his thoughts.'

'What a tragedy that she died so young.'

Vicky nodded.

'For myself—well, I don't feel the loss simply because I never knew her, but Father feels it all the time and it often makes me feel sad.'

Richard's gaze was fixed on his wife's face, his expression an unreadable mask.

'You're a very sweet child,' he murmured unexpectedly. 'You deserve more——' Abruptly he stopped and Vicky shot him an interrogating glance. 'I was going to say that you deserve more than just a father's love; you deserve a mother's love as well.' Richard began to toy with the mushrooms on his plate, but pushed them aside and leant back in his chair. He had finished, and Vicky laid down her knife and fork. She was puzzled, yet admonished herself for suspecting that her husband, when he began to speak, had not intended saying what he had subsequently said.

'I had both a mother's love and a father's,' she told him quietly at length. 'My father gave me both.' Richard said nothing and she added, 'Now I have your love, and this magnificent home'—she spread a hand expressively. —'so what more could any girl want?' She lifted her napkin to dab her lips, and so missed completely the swift action of Richard as for a second he shut his eyes tightly, as if a spasm of excruciating pain had shot through him.

But she did notice the tightness of his mouth, and wanted only to say something that would make him relax, to forget that horrid telephone conversation he had had. Her sweet and tender smile proved to be more than sufficient; he reached across the table to take the small and dainty hand she so eagerly put out to him.

'Oh, but I'm so happy!' she exclaimed. 'I often wonder at what's happened to me, and feel it's all a dream! After all, who am I to be—be ...?' She allowed her voice to trail away, a tinge of colour bringing an adorable glow to her cheeks. Richard, his expression grave but tender, finished softly for her,

'My wife?'

She swallowed, emotion preventing speech for a moment.

'I was really going to say, who am I to be the wife of a man like you?' She had lost her shyness and she met his gaze, noticing the slight frown that had come to his brow. She added then, 'You don't like my looking up to you in the way I do, but, Richard, I'm the kind of girl who must look up to my husband. I've always known that my husband must be honourable in every way ...' Again she allowed her voice to trail off, this time owing to the way in which his eyes had shadowed ... almost as if he were ashamed of something ... 'Is anything the matter?' she asked again, puzzled.

He shook his head; the impression she had had faded on the instant as his reassuring smile broke.

They talked on as the meal progressed, not touching any but light subjects. Sometimes Wallace would come into the conversation and Vicky's expression would become tender. Richard, watching her, seemed to brood now and then, or become preoccupied. But he listened, learning more and more about her father's struggle to attain his goal. He learned that Vicky had for the greater part of her young life been used to comfort and, later, luxury, for Wallace's success had come early, growing and building until that day when, rushing home to the lovely house which he had built a few years previously on the edge of the delightful village of Pressley in Cheshire, he had waved a paper in the air and announced, 'I've made it! I'm a millionaire!'

'It must be very gratifying,' said Richard, breaking into his wife's story at this point, 'to achieve one's ambition through one's own hard work.'

'He always meant to achieve it, and would have gone on and on until he did achieve it. I'm glad he's stopped work now; he should have many years yet in which to enjoy the fruits of his labours.'

A strange unfathomable silence followed during which Richard seemed to withdraw into himself. But presently he said, his voice quiet and finely-modulated, as always,

'I sincerely hope he will have many more years, Vicky. No one in this world deserves it more than he does.'

'He's never thought of marriage,' she said a little regretfully. 'I do have the feeling, sometimes, that he could find someone nice to spend his life with now that I'm married and have left him.' She looked up, her eyes faintly sad. 'He must be lonely, Richard, even though he would deny it if I suggested such a thing.'

'I agree that he must be lonely, and as you say, it would be nice for him if he could find a woman who would be a companion for him.'

'There's Mrs Basset,' mused Vicky, going on to remind Richard that he had met her at their wedding. 'She's nice, isn't she?'

'Yes,' he agreed, 'she is. Has your father known her long?'

'Some years. She once came on holiday with us. I loved it because she played on the sands with me. She's been a widow for years.'

'And yet she's never remarried. She's so attractive that she must have had many opportunities of marrying again.'

'Yes; and she's only young—not yet fifty.'

'She has children, obviously,' said Richard, thinking of the two bridesmaids who were her grandchildren.

'One son, but she doesn't want to live with him and his wife, so she lives on her own in a flat in Macclesfield.'

'Not all that far from here,' mused Richard. 'Her tragedy seems to have been very similar to that of your father.'

'Yes, she was widowed young and left with a child to bring up.'

Richard paused, again becoming thoughtful.

'I take it that your father doesn't see much of Mrs Basset?'

'No, she goes out to work, you see, in an office. I believe she works longer hours than usual in order to earn a little more money. It must be hard for her, having to keep up an establishment. Everything is so expensive these days and people living alone must be very hard-hit.' She was so serious, so mature in her conclusions, that Richard's whole attention was arrested. His expression changed to one of infinite tenderness and a swift smile leapt to her lips.

'I love you,' she said softly, surprising herself even more than him. He made no answer, but merely feasted his eyes on her lovely face. She said after a moment of shyness, 'Do you love me, Richard?' There was no sign of coquetry in her pose, but a hint of archness, mingled with the childish candour in her eyes—which said plainly that her question had really been a statement—was most appealing and Richard found himself swallowing something in his throat, something that was more than mere emotion. He soon collected himself, though, and lifted a quizzical eyebrow as he said,

'Now what, my love, made you ask a question like that?' He rose as he spoke, for they had finished their meal over five minutes ago, and, taking her hand, he brought her to her feet. She quivered in his arms as he took her to his breast, tilting her chin with a gentle finger so that he could kiss her softly-parted lips. 'My beloved ...' He seemed suddenly to change in some unfathomable way, crushing her to him as if he would never let her go. And the kiss he gave her was by no means as gentle as the first—although it thrilled her just as much! 'Well, you haven't answered my question,' he said after a while.

Vicky managed a shaky laugh and said,

'I don't really know what made me ask it.'

'Fibber!' Richard gave her a little shake. 'You were

flirting with me, you tantalising little wretch!'

'Oh, what a horrid thing to say to me!'

'I'll be more horrid if you ever ask me again if I love you!'

'I expect,' mused Vicky not in the least affected by the mock-grimness in his eyes, 'I just wanted to hear you say it.'

Again he shook her, but his lips were seeking her mouth at the same time. She surrendered, carried on the tide of his passion, thrilling to the tenderness of his hands as they came round to cup her firm young breasts.

How lucky she was! And how deliriously happy—so happy, she had told her father, that she was frightened. Vicky leant away from her husband, looked into his eyes and saw the love within their depths ... and she wondered why, at a time like this, she should be recalling the words she had uttered to her father.

CHAPTER FIVE

WALLACE sat on the lawn watching his daughter as she stood by the herbaceous border admiring the glorious show of colour that the weeks of late June and early July had produced. His eyes were narrowed, his thoughts not too happy. Vicky turned, smiled and lifted a hand to him. He beckoned and she came speedily across the velvet carpet that was the pride and joy of Stan, the particular gardener whose task it was to care for it.

'Everything looks so lovely, Father!' Vicky had no idea of the wistful note that edged her voice, but it did not escape her father's keen ears. 'And those trees—I know we had them planted before the house was built, but they look as if they've been there for five or six years!'

'Plenty of good food,' said Wallace, easing himself to a fully upright position on his lounger. 'Tell me, love, how are you liking it, being a great lady?'

She looked down, appearing to become interested in the buckle of her sandal.

'It's rather wonderful—the house, I mean. As for my being a great lady——' she spread her hands deprecatingly, 'that'll never be possible. I am what I am.'

'I had you brought up in the right way, knowing that you'd one day be the daughter of a rich man. That was far-seeing of me, but I don't take full credit for it. I've a special gift for looking to the future and that's how I was able to reach my goal.' His shrewd eyes looked up into her face, a face that was pale yet should not have been. 'What's wrong, my precious?'

She sighed, lost for a moment in thought.

'I don't know,' she answered at last. 'I really don't know.'

The big brown eyes under their bushy brows became narrowed again.

'Richard,' he said, 'he hasn't been able to spend as much time with you lately as he used to, has he?'

'No, he has to work in his study. He does almost all the paperwork himself, as you do.'

'It's a time-consuming task, Vicky. You must try to accept that your husband can't possibly spend all day and every day with you.'

She nodded her head, thinking of the several occasions lately when Richard had dined out, without taking his wife with him. It was business, he had told Vicky, and therefore she would not be happy sitting there while he and his friend talked business. She had naturally asked what kind of business it was, but Richard had managed to evade giving her an answer. Vicky had not mentioned this to her father; he believed that although Richard was away from her all day he did at least spend all his evenings with her.

'I do understand that he has work to do,' she agreed at length.

'You could take up some sort of a hobby,' he suggested thoughtfully.

There was a moment's silence as she pondered this.

'What sort of a hobby, though?'

'You learned to ride exceedingly well at school. You haven't done any riding at all since coming here. I'll tell you what, my pet, I'll get you a nice little mare which you can ride in the shows. How will you like that?'

Her eyes brightened.

'That would be nice, Father. Yes, I would like to ride very much.'

'And now we shall have afternoon tea on the verandah and it'll be like old times, won't it?' Wallace's voice was light, his big eyes twinkling. 'Home-baked scones, fresh butter, jam and cream! Come on, Vicky, we'll have that brought to us in a jiffy!'

She smiled at him with her lovely eyes, tucked her arm in his and together they strolled across the lawn towards the verandah fronting the bungalow. It was hung with flowers, and set out with white garden furniture of the most expensive kind. Vicky settled in a chair, her eyes pensive as she recalled the happy times which she and her father had spent here. The Manor was beautiful, its antiquity appealing to her aesthetically, but of late she had begun to find the very magnitude of the place rather overpowering.

She supposed that, had Richard been with her all the time, then she would never even have noticed that there was anything displeasing about her new home. But as her father had so reasonably pointed out, Richard could not be with her every hour of every day. It would not be a satisfactory arrangement anyway, simply because if he were dancing attendance on his wife all the time then he would be neglecting something else. The Whitethorn estate was incredibly large and in consequence must re-require a great deal of attention. Richard supervised work on the home farm, he saw that the rents came in for the other farms and various properties he owned. He had servants' wages to see to, the ordering of the numerous commodities which were necessary for its smooth running.

He had explained all this to Vicky and she had been quick to understand. It was just those evenings which had upset her since she could not really accept his explanations as satisfactory. She saw no reason why he could not invite these business associates of his to the Manor or, alternatively, ask them to bring their wives to the hotel or wherever the talks took place. Vicky would then be able to accompany him. Also, she could not understand why Richard was so reticent about his absences. The last time she had questioned him about it he had turned a pair of stern cold eyes upon her and in an inexorable tone of voice had said that she would not be interested. That was that. Vicky had not dared to question him further, so severe was his attitude towards her.

Vicky glanced up as her father, having been into the house for the latest copy of *Horse and Hound*, sat down opposite to her.

'I've told Grace we want our tea at once ...' He was already turning the pages of the magazine and Vicky, her lovely eyes fixed on those rather plump hands of his, thought about the years of hard work they had done until, in the end, they had done a great deal in making the million pounds which Wallace maintained he would one day own. 'Here, how does this sound to you? "Thoroughbred mare, ten years. Both parents British National Champions. Regular winner in the show-ring. Most attractive pony. Four white socks, white blaze and white mane and tail. Cutey is for sale only because owner is going abroad. Sensitive horse so good kind home essential". How about that?'

Vicky's eyes were sparkling.

'It sounds perfect for me. How much is it?'

'Oh, that's immaterial——'

'Nothing of the kind,' she interrupted. 'How much, Father?' And when he hesitated, 'I have only to look in the magazine, you know.'

'And if I hide it?' he teased.

'I can go out to Wellsover and buy one.'

'And you would, too! All right: it's one thousand seven hundred pounds.'

'Too much.'

'A fleabite! Besides, you've to think about the horse. She's got to have a good home. If we don't buy her she might not get one.'

Vicky had to laugh.

'You have a way of getting round anything!' she exclaimed. 'All right, Father, we'll have a look at the pony. Where can it be viewed?'

'At a place in Cheshire—Here, take the address down. They haven't given a telephone number; probably don't want people ringing up all the time. I must say, it can be darned annoying.' He handed her a pen from his pocket and she wrote down the address.

'Shall I write off?' she asked, but Wallace shook his head. 'I'll do it. Let's surprise Richard, shall we?'

'Yes, all right.'

'Does he know you can ride?'

'No, as a matter of fact he doesn't. We've never talked about riding, though I know he did ride because I saw him. The horse isn't there now, though. There aren't any horses in the stables at all.'

'I'm aware of that,' he said. 'I shouldn't be buying you the pony if there was a suitable mount in the stables.'

Vicky fell silent for a space, then said with a frown,

'Isn't it strange that a man like Richard hasn't any horses?'

'He didn't need any. One, perhaps,' amended Wallace, 'but if he doesn't ride much then it's an unnecessary expense.'

She darted him a glance of surprise.

'That's a funny thing to say. Richard isn't short of that sort of money.'

'No, I don't suppose he is. However, many big landowners are having to cut their expenses, as I believe I pointed out to you some little while ago.'

She nodded, but nothing more was said on the subject for Grace appeared with the tea tray, which she placed on the table between Wallace and his daughter.

'Anything else, Mr Fraser?'

'No, thank you, Grace.'

'If there is, then don't hesitate to ring. I'm rather busy with your dinner, but not that busy.' Off she went; Vicky giggled while her father grimaced and said,

'She still terrifies me, that one. I feel that "The Amazon of the Cooking Stove" is rather mild. I ought to find a more fitting title for her.'

'I can't really believe she terrifies you, Father. If you thought you'd give her a month's notice then you wouldn't hesitate.'

'Wouldn't I? Let me confess, my child, that I'd give her notice by letter and go away for a month——'

'Rubbish! You haven't got where you are by having cold feet!'

'Oh, well, as I'm not thinking of sacking such an excellent cook let's say no more about it. Just take a sniff at these scones! Fresh from the oven! How does she do it?'

'Cooks them and then puts them back in the oven for a few minutes.'

'Really? I never knew. Bit of a let-down, in a way, isn't it?'

'She could hardly cook fresh scones every time you want them, could she?'

'No, I suppose not. I called for some at one o'clock this morning, and they came just like this.'

'What were you doing up at that time?' she scolded.

'Working, love.' He stopped rather abruptly and there followed a momentary silence. Vicky, sensing something strange about his manner, subjected him to a penetrating stare, but read nothing from his fixed expression. 'I've a great deal of tidying up to do—with regard to the business, of course.'

'You're not giving up?'

'Well ... I have thought about it. Now that you're settled in that stately home I've always had in mind for you I haven't any more ambitions of any great importance. So I might round it all up and retire.'

'I can't believe it. You're only young, Father—not anywhere near sixty yet.'

He smiled faintly at that and reminded her that he was on the wrong side of fifty.

'I'd like a few years of retirement, just to enjoy some of what I've made.'

'You should be enjoying *all* of what you've made. Why not go on one of these fantastic world cruises we read about?'

'You wouldn't miss me?' Something strange here, too, she thought. It was almost as if he were fishing for information, as he himself would have put it, almost as if he were seeking for reassurance that she was so contented and happy in her new life that she would not miss him.

'That,' she said chidingly, 'is a silly question and you know it.'

He gave a deep sigh.

'Vicky, my precious child, I want nothing more than that you are perfectly happy. Are you, dear?'

The anxiety was plain to see; Vicky blamed herself for the rather depressed way she had behaved on these last two or three visits. She must not cause her father anxiety again.

'I'm as happy as it's possible to be, Father.'

'Truly?'

'Truly. And now if you don't tackle those scones at once they'll have to go into the oven yet again—unless you want to eat them cold, of course!'

Vicky and Wallace both fell in love with Cutey, and as she seemed to take to them everyone was satisfied. Vicky rode her, found no faults with her, though of course she did not try her over the jumps.

'She's lovely!' exclaimed Vicky, feeling excited at the prospect of owning her. She was excited too at the thought of what Richard would say. He would be bound to like the pony and to approve of the purchase. In all probability, mused Vicky, he would buy himself another horse so that he and she could ride together, over the estate lands and perhaps across the moors.

The pony was delivered to the bungalow where it remained in one of the paddocks, as Vicky did not know which field her husband would want to have it put in. There were paddocks, of course, but these had cows in them at present.

She watched Richard striding across the fields, her excitement growing with every step that brought him nearer to her.

'I've a surprise for you!' she exclaimed when eventually he was with her as she stood framed in the front doorway.

'Have you, my love?' Richard bent to kiss her, then sent her a questioning glance. 'What is this surprise? If you've been transforming my study into a cosy sitting-room then I'll warn you here and now that I shan't be pleased about it.'

She laughed lightly, aware as always of his magnetic personality, of the way his presence heightened her emotions ... of her deep love for him but also of a yearning which she had long since given up trying to understand.

'Father's bought me a horse!'

'A ...?' Instead of the look of approval and interest which she expected Vicky was shocked to see her husband's face tighten, his mouth compress. And even his voice shocked her, so harsh and cold was it as he said, 'A horse? What sort? If I know your father it won't be a fifty-pound hack he's bought.'

Vicky stepped back, pressing her hands to her breast. She knew her face had paled, that her eyes had misted up.

'Father wouldn't buy a hack, no, of course he wouldn't——'

'How much did he pay for this horse?'

'One thousand seven hundred,' she faltered, aware as soon as she spoke that she should have hesitated.

'Flaunting his money!' Two streaks of crimson crept along the sides of his mouth, a mouth that had become so thin it was more than a cruel line. He seemed to be quivering with fury and, bewildered by this dramatic and terrifying change in her husband, Vicky automatically took another step backwards, an action that seemed to incense him even more than he was incensed already. He followed her, slamming the front door to behind him. 'Where is this horse?' he demanded, towering above her in a menacing attitude. 'Where is it, I say!'

Vicky swallowed, the tears filling her eyes and dropping on to her white cheeks.

'At the b-bungalow—in one of the—the p-paddocks.'

'Then that's where it stays! I've endured more than enough of your father's——' He stopped abruptly, turning away. 'I'm sorry,' he said hoarsely. 'Forgive me, Vicky ...' He came round, collecting himself, but she sensed that anger still smouldered beneath the surface.

'I'm sorry, dear,' he said again. 'I'll go over with you afterwards and take a look at your pony.'

Vicky stared up at him through a mist of tears.

'Richard ... what have I done? I th-thought you'd be pl-pleased——' Her head dropped into her hands and she sobbed as if her heart would break. Richard, hesitating for a moment, a look of angry resignation on his face, stared down at her bent head. Her hair, falling on either side of her face, left the back of her neck bare; he put out a hand and covered it, murmuring to her in tones that seemed to break with despair.

'My dear, don't cry. I shouldn't have hurt you——'

'Why did you?' she cried. 'Why were you so angry?'

For a moment he could not answer, and when he did it was merely to say, on a deep, sigh,

'You wouldn't understand, Vicky dear,' and he turned her round, took a handkerchief from his pocket and gently dried her cheeks. Her sobs continued, racking her slender body so that it jerked spasmodically against him. 'My dear, don't upset yourself like this.' He paused a moment as if trying to find something to say by way of an excuse for his earlier conduct. 'I've had a trying day, my love, so do please forgive me.'

'A trying day?' She looked up, her eyes still filled with tears. 'Oh, I'm sorry. Did something go wrong?'

He nodded his head.

'Yes, dear, it did, but that was no reason why I should have lost my temper with you.' His gaze was tender as he looked into her eyes; she was reassured, but only to some extent, and a frown knit his brow. He bent and kissed her, tenderly, passionately ... but she still was not fully reassured. 'Would you like us to go over to the bungalow before dinner, or afterwards? It will still be daylight even if we go afterwards.'

'I don't mind,' she answered dully, all the pleasure of

owning the pony blotted out by the scene just enacted. Doubts had been gradually creeping into her mind, doubts that had begun as mere threads of uneasiness, and for which she had been unable to find a cause, but now her doubts were growing, gaining strength, though she was still mystified as to their origin. 'I think,' she murmured presently, 'we'd better go after dinner. I couldn't let my father see that I'd been crying.'

'No, we definitely mustn't let him see that!' Richard spoke with emphasis, shaking his head. 'We'll go over after dinner, then. Are you going to phone him?'

'Yes.' Vicky paused, examining his face, noting the greyness about it, the dark and brooding expression in his eyes. 'Richard ...'

'Yes, darling?'

'Do you really want to go? I mean, if you've had a bad day, a tiring one, then please don't feel you must go over to look at the pony. We can go tomorrow evening.'

But Richard was already shaking his head.

'You're wanting to show it to me, which is only natural. Besides,' he added, turning slightly so that his expression was hidden from her, 'I've to go out tomorrow evening—in fact, I shall be out for most of the day.'

'I see ...' Vicky spoke after a long, profound silence. 'It's a—a business matter, of course.' Her heart had sunk right into her feet. 'Will you not be—be——' She stopped, swallowing convulsively in an attempt to clear the blockage in her throat. 'Will you not be in for lunch, then?'

'No, Vicky, I'm afraid not.' She said nothing; it was taking her all her time to prevent herself from bursting into a renewed flood of weeping. 'Perhaps you'd like to spend the day with your father?'

She nodded listlessly.

'Yes, I think I shall do that.' She looked up at him, a

core of misery at her heart. 'I'll leave you now, Richard, so you can rest before dinner.' She spoke mechanically, turning away, only to stumble as she began to walk towards the stairs. Richard's voice seemed a long way off as he asked her if she was all right. She made no answer and he was suddenly beside her, but she raised a hand, warding him off even before he had touched her. 'Yes, I'm quite all right, Richard. I'll see you at dinner.'

It was only to be expected that the meal was eaten in an atmosphere of strain. Several times Richard, plainly regretting his angry outburst, attempted to draw his wife into conversation, but as her contribution was nothing more than monosyllabic responses to his questions, he soon abandoned his efforts and lapsed into silence. But when at last the meal was over and it was time for them to go to the bungalow Vicky brightened up, determined not to let Wallace guess that she was unhappy.

'Ah!' he greeted them jovially as they got out of the car, Richard having decided that, as the sky was overcast and rain might be expected, they had better not risk walking, since it was about a quarter of a mile between the bungalow and the Manor itself. 'Come to give your opinion on the pony, eh, Richard?' Although he spoke to his son-in-law Wallace's eyes were on his daughter's face. She smiled brightly and tucked her hand into her husband's.

'Yes, Father,' she answered before Richard could speak. 'Has she been good?'

'She could scarcely be anything else, there in the paddock all by herself. I've been out to her once or twice; she's a friendly animal but wants companionship. How about buying a nice Arab stallion to keep her company, Richard?'

'Not at present,' curtly and with an inexorable inflection to Richard's voice. 'Later, maybe.'

'You could have one,' persisted Wallace. 'You know very well you could. What's the objection?'

Richard turned to him, his grey eyes narrowed almost to slits.

'No objection, Wallace, merely caution.'

Caution ... Vicky glanced from her husband to Wallace, then back again. What could Richard mean by that? she wondered. Wallace had lowered his eyes, and he gave a gentle kick at one of the tyres, as though he had suddenly noticed something there. Richard moved away from the car and the other two followed.

'Which paddock is the horse in?' he wanted to know, glancing around and taking in the immaculate vista of smooth lawns, weedless flower borders and a shrubbery bright with colour. Away in the distance ranged the mountains, dappled with gold as the long rays of the lowering sun spread their translucent glory over their summits. His eyes returned to the scene immediately around him and he gave a small sigh, a sigh which his wife heard and which went straight to her heart. Richard was unhappy—desperately so. Instinctively she knew it ... and she had known it for some time ...

Distressed, she looked up into his dark face, wishing even yet again that she could come to regard herself as his equal. It was no fault of his that she had this inferiority complex; he had never, either by word or look, given her one little hint that he considered himself above her. If she *could* rid herself of this feeling of inferiority then she would automatically break the barrier that kept her from insisting on sharing his troubles with him. But she possessed these inhibitions and at times they tended to warp her vision, which was what happened now as she said to herself,

'I'm not good enough for him; I'm a nobody while he's

an aristocrat.' The admission only strengthened the doubts that had been increasing in her mind. Richard, admitting that she was beautiful, had been carried away by that beauty, but now he could see his mistake, could see that his wife was far beneath him. That, decided Vicky, was the reason why he had not invited his business associates to dine at the Manor, and why he had never allowed Vicky to accompany him when he went out to dine.

'She's in the far paddock, Richard.' Wallace's voice answering her husband's question interrupted Vicky's unhappy musings and she lifted her head, producing a bright expression just for her father's benefit. His dream, his burning ambition, his final aim in life, had been to see her married to a gentleman of quality. His dream had come true and Vicky vowed that nothing she herself ever did would shatter that dream for him.

And so she actually tripped along in front of the two men as they all made their way to the far paddock, a lush green enclosure in which Cutey was cropping the grass. She called and the pony came with a trot to the fence.

'You darling!' She patted her neck, turning to remark on the distinctive effect of the pony's colouring. 'Well, darling,' she said, shining up at her husband, 'what do you think of her?'

Instead of answering immediately Richard appeared to be fully absorbed by the miraculous change in his wife's demeanour. At dinner she had been definitely morose; on the way here she had become a little more cheerful in preparation for the meeting with her father, but now she was undeniably gay, and as she watched his expression Vicky knew that he was more than a little baffled by the change in her.

'She's a real beauty,' he admitted, patting the mare's

silky neck. 'You were lucky, Wallace. This horse will be excellent to breed from.'

'I'm not breeding from her,' put in Vicky at once. 'I'm intending to ride her in shows—just locally, of course.'

'You never told me you were an experienced rider, Vicky,' said her husband in surprise.

'I learnt at school. I'm not very good, really, but I enjoy riding and I believe I can do some eventing with Cutey here.'

Richard seemed to become inordinately interested in her for a moment, his grey eyes darting from her to the horse, then back again, as if he were mentally assessing their worth as potential winners.

'So you don't see any major faults in her?' Wallace was asking. 'I didn't think you would.'

'You know about horses, then?'

'A little, so don't look so surprised, lad. I was persuaded to buy a racehorse once, but as the venture very swiftly began to make a loss I withdrew. It wasn't my intention to become involved in anything that wasn't going to show me a profit.'

Vicky, a little perturbed by her father's calling Richard 'lad', looked rather anxiously at her husband, but if he were annoyed by it he gave no sign as he remarked dryly,

'No, I don't suppose you would become involved in anything that didn't show a profit ... either financially or otherwise.'

'Otherwise?' echoed Vicky. 'What do you mean, Richard? Profits always refer to money, surely.'

'Not always, my dear,' her husband argued, his voice as expressionless as his face. 'It's quite possible to profit in other ways than by the increase of one's capital.'

'Shall we go into the house?' suggested Wallace with what seemed unnecessary abruptness. 'We'll have a drink before you leave. Vicky, shall you come over tomorrow and collect Cutey?'

'Yes—er—I'd like to spend the day with you if you're not going to be too busy. Richard has to go somewhere on business and won't be at home for lunch.' Her voice was light; she knew that Richard had guessed why she had not included dinner when talking about his absence form home.

'So you'll be dining alone?' he was saying in the car as he drove her home about an hour later.

'Yes, I couldn't let Father know that you were dining out.'

'I've dined out before. Doesn't he know about those occasions?'

Vicky shook her head in the darkness.

'No; I shan't ever tell him, either.' Something chill in her voice made him turn and slant her a quesioning glance. 'I find no profit in worrying him with such things.'

'I see ...' A silence fell. Vicky stared in front of her, only vaguely aware of the beauty of the mountains as, with the twilight having faded, the peaks were now soft-ened by subtle shades of purple and grey, with the sheen of pearl reflecting on them from a crescent moon that had escaped from the rolling clouds which every now and then would mask its light. The high moorlands were drowsy, silent and primitive, lonely as they had been be-fore the coming of man.

'Vicky dear ...' Richard's voice came softly to her ears as he turned the car into the long avenue leading to the Manor. 'Is anything troubling you?'

Why did he ask, and in such a strained and guilty tone of voice.

'No, nothing,' she answered, injecting a note of sur-prise into her voice. 'What a strange thing to say, Rich-ard.'

'Is it, my darling, after I've been so unreasonably un-kind to you?'

Her lip quivered as the memory of his unkindness brought it all vividly back to her. She said, suddenly de-termined never to let him see just how much she had been hurt,

'It was nothing. You explained that you'd had a troublesome day, so it was excusable——'

'On the contrary,' he interrupted shortly, 'it was not excusable. Vicky, my love, say you forgive me.'

There was no humility in his voice, she realised. No, rather was it faintly arrogant, as if he were demanding an apology, demanding it as his right! A little wearily she said yes, she forgave him.

Half an hour later she was in his arms, her body close to his as they stood in her bedroom, where she had waited breathlessly, a rising, choking desolate fear slowly en-gulfing her as, with each moment that passed, she became more and more convinced that her husband would not come to her. And then the door had opened and her heart seemed to lurch right up into her throat before settling again to a calmness that seemed like heaven after the emotional strain of the past five minutes or so. She ran to him, her dainty nightgown flowing out, then back again to cling fleetingly to her tender form. With a little catch of his breath Richard caught her in his arms and crushed her to him. Every fear dissolved under the pas-sionate domination of his kisses, for they were tender too, and his voice was infinitely reassuring as he said, his lips close to her breast,

'My love ... my darling little wife ... I'll never hurt you again.' She was swung into his arms and carried to the big four-poster bed, her strong young arms about his neck, her eager lips awaiting his, just as every nerve in her body awaited the fire of his lovemaking that would take her to the very heights of ecstasy.

'I love you so,' she murmured happily. 'Oh, Richard, I was so afraid you wouldn't come to me!'

'Beloved!' His voice, vibrant and masterful, was yet gentle and tender, as was the way he dropped one shoulder strap and took her breast in his hand. His lips found hers, sensual lips that, unlike the touch of his hand, knew no mercy as they crushed her soft and yielding mouth in a kiss that bruised even while it brought a glow of happiness to her eyes. 'You must never be afraid again, my darling,' he murmured hoarsely when at last he took his lips from hers. 'I shall always come to you! How could I keep away from such seductive beauty as yours?' His hands moved; the nightgown was brought down to her waist, then further. Richard put out a hand to the bed light, and the room was plunged into darkness, except for the argent glow of the crescent moon entering through a small parting in the window drapes.

CHAPTER SIX

Two weeks went by, weeks of such undiluted happiness for Vicky that she often wondered if she had imagined those previous doubts, for they were now as remote as the sun in a cloud-darkened sky. She had been practising on Cutey; Richard had had some jumps erected for her in a large flat field. He had had the grass cut short, to make the conditions ideal for her.

'You deserve it, my darling,' he had said when she thanked him. 'Nothing is too good for you.' He was still busy during the daytime and Vicky often rode over to the bungalow.

'I'm so happy that I'm frightened,' she told her father, who immediately reminded her that she had said something of the kind before. But he added before she could comment,

'There was a time, about a fortnight ago, when I suspected you were not feeling as happy as you ought. I was wrong, obviously.'

'Yes,' she lied, 'you were.'

The small car she had asked for had been ordered before there was any question of her marriage to Richard, and although she and her father had mentioned this to Richard, Vicky rather thought that it had not really registered in his mind, and he had seemed preoccupied on both occasions. There was a wait for delivery of six months but it arrived at last and Vicky went with her father to collect it from a garage in Buxton. Although small, it was expensive, with sporty lines and a bright exterior finish of gold metallic paint.

'You look as if you were born in that seat,' declared the salesman laughingly. 'I don't think I've ever seen anyone look so comfortable when handling a new car for the first time.'

'I certainly feel very much more comfortable than behind the wheel of that,' she said, pointing to the Rolls in which her father had driven her into town. The salesman grimaced, and prudently kept to himself the thought that it was just like a woman to show total indifference to the superlative engineering qualities of the Rolls-Royce car. 'Is it all ready to drive away?' she asked after making a second adjustment to the seat. She had been out in it, just for a few minutes, and she was now eager to drive it to the Manor and let her husband see it.

'Yes, it's all okay.'

'I'll follow you, Father.'

They stopped at the bungalow for afternoon tea, then Vicky drove home. Richard was in the forecourt when she arrived; she saw his eyes darken in a sudden frown after the first initial flash of puzzlement.

'My car!' she cried, as she jumped out. 'What do you think of it, Richard? Isn't it a lovely colour?' Her hair was a little untidy, sent awry by the breeze blowing through the open window of the car; her cheeks were flushed, her eyes sparkling with pleasure and with anticipation. She wanted Richard to say at once that he would like to try it out. Instead, he just stood for a long moment, staring in silence at the shining new model which his wife had so proudly parked on the forecourt.

'Very nice,' he said tautly at last. That was all. Vicky, his indifference a most efficient damper on her spirits, stood before him, looking up at a pair of hard cold eyes, a mouth that was compressed into a thin harsh line. Like a flash another scene came back to her, the scene when she had told him about the pony. She heard again Richard's furious words,

'I've endured more than enough of your father's——'

He had stopped; Vicky in her state of bleak unhappiness had not given this any depth of thought until later, and even then she refrained from asking Richard what he had meant. Far better to leave it, she decided, especially as she and Richard were so blissfully happy. Now, however, as the words came to her, she found no difficulty in finishing off the sentence which had been cut. At least she knew the gist of what had been left out, since it tied up with what he had said initially. Richard had endured more than enough of her father's flaunting of his wealth. But did that make sense? Her father had never flaunted his wealth. The pony was not as expensive as it could have been, so why had Richard taken exception to her having the pony as a present from her father? Did Richard consider that as Vicky was his wife then it ought to have been he who had the privilege of buying the more costly presents for her? Yes, that certainly could be the explanation, decided Vicky.

'Should Father not have bought this car for me, Richard?'

A cold unfriendly silence and then,

'He has a right to buy you anything he wants to buy you.'

'The car was ordered even before you and I had met,' she said gently and, when he maintained his austere silence, 'I thought you would be as happy as I—and want to go for a run in it right away.' Her eyes misted up; it was fast being borne in upon her that her husband was a man of moods . . . and some of those moods could cause her excruciating pain.

'We'll go for a run in it later,' he promised, and although his voice had softened slightly, there was now a hint of bitterness to be detected in it.

The following day Vicky decided to go to Buxton to do some shopping. She drove in, parked her car, then, after buying all the items for which she came, she decided to have a cup of tea, and walked up the main street to her favourite café. No sooner had she sat down than a voice she recognised hailed her and she turned to look up into the frank and smiling face of John Bailey.

'So we meet again, Mrs Sherrand! May I join you? I noticed you haven't ordered yet.'

'Yes, of course.' Vicky indicated the chair opposite to her. 'Join me by all means.' He sat down, beckoning to the waitress.

'What are you having. Tea and sticky buns?'

'Tea and scones, please.'

'I expect,' he said when the waitress had gone, 'that you're wondering why I'm up in these parts again?' Vicky merely nodded and he continued, 'I've some other land to look at—not anywhere near yours, so don't panic about your view or anything like that.'

'Which land is it?' inquired Vicky curiously.

'Belongs to an old lady by the name of Mrs Sarah Austin. Do you know her?'

Vicky blinked, shaking her head mechanically. She had heard that Louisa Austin, Richard's old flame, had an aged aunt somewhere around these parts.

'I haven't ever met her,' she answered.

'No? Well, she's getting on in years and has decided to sell out and make her money over to a niece—or was it a nephew? Doesn't matter; all we're interested in is the land.'

'You still intend to build an estate?'

'That's the idea.'

'There's no work around these parts. It's mainly wild uninhabited moorland supporting sheep.'

'Then we shall have to build a trading estate.' He glanced up, leaning back as the waitress came up with the tray. 'It was a funny business about your land, wasn't it? Some mix-up, apparently, because the land definitely was for sale, but quite unexpectedly it was withdrawn. Your husband came into money—so the boss told me. I'll bet you're most relieved, Mrs Sherrand, that your estate's going to remain intact?'

Vicky said nothing; she was thoughtfully going over the information which had just been imparted to her. It was plain that Richard had been under severe financial difficulties, and he had put up a large amount of land for sale. It seemed to Vicky as she pondered the matter that the sale of the land which formed her father's estate had been a preliminary to a much larger sale. Had Richard hoped that this first sale could extricate him from his difficulties? This certainly seemed a feasible explanation for the sale of that first parcel of land. Obviously it had not done for Richard's finances what he had hoped, hence the putting up of more land for sale. Then, most opportunely indeed, Richard had come into money. Had he inherited it? Vicky wondered, again fervently wishing that her relationship with her husband were such that she could ask him to take her into his confidence. But their relationship in that respect was still not intimate and Vicky continued to blame herself, since, despite the fact that she and Richard were blissfully happy together, she still had that inferiority complex regarding his background and her own. In consequence, she had never marshalled the courage to question him too closely about his private affairs.

John Bailey was speaking again, saying something about his colleague not turning up.

'Your colleague?' blinked Vicky, brought from her reverie. 'Er—I didn't catch what you said? I'm sorry; I was miles away.'

'There are two of us this time. Danny left me a couple of hours ago saying he'd better get some information from the Surveyor's Office here in Buxton. Said he'd meet me at half-past three, but I waited till four at the appointed place. I suppose this café would have been a more sensible rendezvous.'

'How will you contact him, then? Did you come in one car or two?'

'One. I expect he'll be in the car when I get back to the car park. I did say I'd park on the one by the hotel, and as he's got a key he'll be all right.'

Twenty minutes later Vicky, having said goodbye to the young man, was making her way to the park on which she had left her own car. Now and then she stopped to window-gaze, since there was no hurry for her to get home. And it was while she was looking in the window of a dress shop in a rather crowded part of the main street that she heard John's voice again.

'Danny—so there you are! I was just going to see if you were in the car.' Vicky soon realised that the men had both stopped on coming upon one another and she was just about to turn her head when Danny's voice came to her.

'I've done all I set out to do. And by the way, I got the full explanation for the withdrawal of that Sherrand land. He married money, apparently! Did it all in a great hurry; the girl's father's a millionaire and he settled all Sherrand's debts ...' The men were moving on; Danny's voice was lost in the press of people, and in the increasing distance between him and Vicky who, rooted to the spot, could not have turned now had she wanted to.

Married money ... The two words hammered in

Vicky's mind, louder and louder until she actually put her hands to her ears. Married money ... So much explained. She closed her eyes tightly, crucified by the knowledge that she had been used—by Richard to remedy his financial difficulties and by Wallace to realise his dream. How had Wallace engineered it, though?

The answer was not long in coming; Vicky remembered with growing bitterness how he had invited Richard over to dine with them, evading the questions which Vicky in her curiosity had put to him regarding his reason for the invitation. Wallace must have known of Richard's desperate situation—but looking at it now Vicky wondered why she herself had not grasped the fact that something must be wrong when, in the first place, Richard had sold land to her father. At the time she had not given the matter much thought at all, since she was so used to her father negotiating for, and buying land; his business depended on his ability to avail himself of land. All she had considered at the time was that the situation for the proposed bungalow was idyllic, and that they were fortunate indeed to have the privilege of living, in effect, on the Whitethorn estate, which was known to be one of the largest and most beautiful in the county.

At last Vicky managed to move, automatically making her way through the scurry of people who were now coming from offices and shops, impatient to get home. She was unable to think clearly any more; it seemed as if she were suspended in an emotional vacuum, as if nature were affording her a respite from the agony of mind which had come to her as a result of what she had overheard.

How she got to her car she never knew; she merely found herself there, unlocking the door, getting in, switching on the ignition.

Married money ... Did it in a great hurry ... her father's a millionaire and he settled all Sherrand's debts ...

Yes, thought Vicky with a shuddering sigh that racked her whole body, so much explained, and without the least difficulty at all.

She drove home, lost in the vacuum again. She had not the mental skill to bring her thoughts to function properly; she did not wish them to function, for in this dazed state no real pain was felt, just a dull ache germinated by despair.

Reaching home at last, she put the car away in the garage Richard had given her, then walked into the hall and climbed the stairs. It was all mechanical, as if some clockwork device were directing her every action. But, once in her lovely bedroom, with its exquisite antique furniture, its Sèvres dressing-table set ... its four-poster bed, all restraint left her and she put her face in her hands and wept convulsively.

Her husband did not love her—had never loved her. Yet he could take her money for his comfort and her body for his pleasure. Vicky shuddered at this latter idea, cringing with shame at the memory of her own eager surrender to the mastery of his ardour. She felt tainted, unclean because she had been made love to without love. What kind of a man was he? That he was totally without principle or pride was an undisputed fact. Her idol had feet of clay ...

Naturally, after a moment, Vicky's thoughts switched to her father, whose ambition had become an obsession which she had tried in vain to destroy. That he could marry her off to someone who did not love her was something she could scarcely believe, and she wandered around the matter, her thoughts becoming so muddled that she found no logic in them at all until, resignedly, she had to accept that her father had in fact sacrificed her for the realisation of his dream.

At last she dragged herself from the deluge of misery that engulfed her; she could not weep for ever, life must go on. And, strangely, her first thought was for her father. She remembered all the years of love he had lavished on her, his unsparing outlay of expenditure for her well-being and her education. He must never guess that his machinations had been made known to her, that the realisation of his dream had brought her to the very depths of misery. She thought she could understand to some extent the driving force that had been responsible for his action. All his life he had succeeded in whatever he set out to accomplish; he could never have tolerated failure of his final and most pressing dream, and had not Vicky married Richard then Wallace would have continued to scheme until that dream became a reality. That was his nature, the influence of inherited traits; he was not wholly to blame for the way in which those inherited traits drove him.

Vicky's tears flowed again, because in spite of her understanding, there was no doubt that her father had done her a heartbreaking disservice when he encouraged the attentions of Richard. Shame burned once again within her as she pictured her husband, coldly and calculatingly talking 'business' with her father, accepting the bargain offered to him.

And she, in her innocence and complete trust, had believed that Richard had fallen in love with her. She recalled teasing her father about it, saying that, after all his scheming, the marriage he had wanted had come about quite naturally, without his aid.

He had said nothing, she remembered, and he had

deliberately avoided meeting her gaze.

He had known that she was in love with Richard and Vicky was in no doubt at all that he had informed Richard of this. She could see her father, anxious but determined, telling Richard emphatically that he must never allow Vicky to learn that he did not love her.

To give Richard his due, he had tried hard in his pretence of loving her, treating her with infinite gentleness, speaking to her tenderly, taking such care of her. How well he had done it! If he were an experienced actor he could not have improved on the convincing role of tender lover that he had adopted. No bride could have had more thought lavished on her, more tender words whispered in her ear, more reverence and respect in the caresses of her husband. Yes, he had acted his part so well that she had been completely taken in. True, there had been moments of uneasiness, when she had been conscious of something missing in their relationship, but she had blamed herself, because she had this inferiority complex and believed she always would have it.

That Richard regretted his marriage now seemed to be evident. He was unhappy; Vicky had known it from his drawn and grey countenance on more than one occasion. Well, for her he could have his freedom, but there was her father to think about. A divorce would break him, especially as he would be faced with the knowledge that he himself was to blame for her broken life. He had done wrong, but Richard was the real aggressor, having been interested solely in marrying for money, accepting a dowry, in fact. And it must have been a fantastically large one, Vicky was thinking, since if it was only a moderate sum of money Richard needed, he could have raised it, surely, in some other way.

A movement in the other room alerted her to the fact

that her face was wet with tears, that her eyes must be puffed up, that her forehead was wet with perspiration. She ran into the bathroom and locked the door, listening for the centre door to open.

'Vicky, my love.' Richard's voice, tender and low; she realised that the door had been opened noiselessly.

'I'm having a bath,' she called.

'Can I come in? I haven't kissed you since this morning, remember.'

'No, sorry. I'm in the bath and can't reach the door.' The lie came easily from her lips, amazing her.

'I can't for the life of me see why you had the need to lock it. You never have before.'

'Sorry,' she said again, standing by the wash-hand basin, her clenched fists pressed to her heart. If she had not learned what she had she would now be in his arms, responding to kisses that thrilled her, setting her emotions on fire so that she yearned for more than the mastery of his lips. 'I'll—I'll be out soon.'

'How long must I wait?'

What spuriousness!

'Half an hour, perhaps——'

'Half——' How long have you been in there, for goodness' sake?'

'Not very long.' At least that was the truth.

'I do believe you're teasing me, my love. I shall give you ten minutes. That's an order; understand?' So imperious his voice. A few short hours ago it would have given her pleasure to take an order from her husband.

Ten minutes ... She glanced in the huge oval mirror almost covering the centre of the wall above the bath. How could she erase the evidence of her tears in so short a time? For a moment she toyed with the idea of going out and having a showdown with him, but she was reluctant to do so until she had given herself time to think rationally about the outcome of such an action on her part. As yet she had had not time at all, since her mind was still partly dazed by the disillusionment she had suffered in the discovery that Richard did not love her. Perhaps he still loved Louisa Austin ... The idea had no sooner come to her than she was asking herself another question: where did Richard go on those evenings when he went out to dine? Was he really with business associates? What kind of business did they discuss, anyway? If it had been Wallace then there might have been an easy explanation, but there was no such easy explanation regarding Richard's 'business dinners'.

Was he with Louisa, the girl he would have married had *her* father been able—and willing—to settle his debts? Swiftly on this thought Vicky was recalling what John Bailey had said about Louisa's aunt having decided to sell all her land and make the money over to her niece.

Vicky closed her eyes tightly, giving a little moan as a pain shot right through her head. Someone had declared, many years ago, that she was the kind of a girl to be 'put on', and this had certainly been proved correct. Her thoughts switched again to Louisa Austin, who was going to be rich once her aunt's money came to her ...

Richard's voice was heard again, still imperious.

'Vicky, you're so quiet I'm beginning to wonder if you are in the bath. I had an idea you were in your room when I first entered mine.'

'I'm in the bath now,' called Vicky, conscious of the clamminess of her forehead and her hands, clenched tightly as they were. She felt ill suddenly, ill and lost and helpless. Never had she experienced the feeling of aloneness; always she had had her father, a prop both strong and stout. But now she felt utterly alone, deserted, ill-

used, despised even, since she was convinced that Richard, beneath the veneer of loving tenderness which he
showed to her, secretly despised her, considering her far
beneath him.

'Is anything wrong, dear?' His voice with its assumed
concern was like sandpaper on a nerve. She spoke
sharply, saying no, there was nothing wrong.

'I'll be out soon,' she added. 'Please go away, Richard.'

She heard a long-drawn-out sigh before the quiet
muffled sound of his shoes on the thick-pile carpet.

Vicky ran some water into the bath, some more into the
wash-bowl so that she could bathe her face and eyes.
After drying her face by gently dabbing it with the towel,
she poured scented bath fluid into the water, then released the plug, allowing the water to run from the bath.
Steam had risen to cover the mirrors, a circumstance for
which she was glad since, as she emerged from the bathroom, her husband glanced over her shoulder, as if to
settle a doubt in his mind that she really had been in the
bath. His eyes moved over her, though, and she did
wonder if he were thinking that it was most odd that she
should have dressed in the steamy bathroom instead of
the bedroom, as was her usual practice.

'Have you been crying?' he asked, frowning as his
eyes settled on her face.

'No,' she lied badly. 'But I got the bath liquid in my
eyes and I'm afraid it's made them red.'

'You silly child. How did you manage that?'

'I don't know, Richard. It just happened.' Glibly
though the lie came, Vicky, totally unused to such
speciousness, could not bring herself to meet her husband's gaze. He reached out to take her hand, drawing
her to him with tender gentle movements.

'Let me kiss you, my darling.' He tilted her face,

frowned again at the heightened colour of her cheeks, but made no comment as he bent to kiss her quivering lips. Then he held her at arms' length, his penetrating eyes all-examining. 'Something is wrong, Vicky,' he declared at length. 'What is it? Where have you been today?'

'Into town. I needed to do some shopping.'

'You drove yourself in?'

She nodded, recalling how pleasurable had been the idea of driving her new car, despite the poor reception it had had—initially—from her husband. Later he had tried it out, taking the wheel and driving fast. He had praised its performance, had been his usual charming self as he told Vicky that she was a very lucky girl. Her dejection had faded then, and when eventually the car was in the garage and they were coming away she had tucked her arm into his, shone up at him with her big grey-green eyes and said happily,

'Thank you for liking my car, Richard. I would never have taken to it if you hadn't.'

He had smiled at her in that tender way of his, and he was smiling at her in the same way now, as she stood before him, imprisoned by the hold he had on her arms.

'Yes,' she said, 'I drove myself in. I would have gone over to the bungalow and perhaps asked Father if he wanted to go into town—in which case we'd have gone in his car. But I changed my mind, knowing he'd be busy.' She paused a moment; she had been intending to tell Richard, merely as a natural follow-up to what she had been saying, that her father was considering winding up his business and retiring. But somehow she wanted to hold back the information, remembering that Richard had confided very little of his private affairs to her. And because of this he had put a distance between them, a sort of gap that Vicky herself had widened owing to the inferiority complex she had allowed to take possession of her. No, she decided, she would not tell Richard of her father's half-made decision to retire. What had it to do with him anyway?

CHAPTER SEVEN

THE emotional vacuum into which Vicky had drifted on that fateful afternoon when she overheard John Bailey and his friend talking seemed to have dropped upon her again, this time to find some permanency. She had no idea what she wanted to do as regarded the knowledge that had come to her; on the one hand she was tempted to have a showdown with her husband, but immediately upon this half-formed idea would come the thought of her father, and the probable repercussions that could mar his happiness to such an extent that he would never recover. He had worked so hard, unceasingly for over forty years, and now he was reaping the reward of those labours. He had his house, his car, his leisure to a certain extent . . . and he had the satisfaction of knowing that the daughter whom he had deliberately fitted for the role of a lady of quality had become the mistress of a stately home. How could she bring all this to naught? Her father had given all and asked nothing in return. He had received his daughter's love in abundance, but what price that love if she were now to forget it in her desire to hit back at the man who had so callously entered into so nefarious a bargain as that offered to him by her father? No, she could not destroy her father's peace of mind, Vicky finally decided. And so the result was that she had of necessity to act a part in her relationship with her husband.

Three weeks went by and she was gradually becoming used to the deceit she was practising. But she often wondered how it was that she could respond to Richard's lovemaking with much the same eagerness and willing surrender as before. She supposed it was the strength of her own love that carried her through, for although she now had no real respect for Richard, she still loved him with all her heart. Her love would never die; this she knew, and accepted in the same way that she accepted that her husband did *not* love her, and never would do so.

She tried to fill her daily life with activities which would leave her little time for thinking—but of course it was impossible. To have reached the heights of happiness and then to learn that she merely lived in a fool's paradise was not something that could be lightly thrust to the back of her mind as if it were a matter of no consequence. However, she did manage to find an interest, the hobby which her father had in mind when he bought her the pony. She joined the riding-club and was immediately entered for several forthcoming events, not least of which was the Handford Championship. It was when she was talking to Trudie, a friend she had made at the riding-club, that she learned that Louisa Austin was to be one of her competitors.

'She's good,' warned Trudie. 'She usually takes everything before her at the local gymkhanas.'

'She rides here?'

'Everwhere.'

Vicky did not know why she should have been secretive with Richard over the show. She vaguely realised that he must learn eventually that she was riding in it, but for some reason she kept the news from him for the time being.

He was always interested in her riding and would stand watching her practising over the jumps and praise her efficient handling of Cutey.

'She's no trouble,' Vicky told him one day as she came

towards the fence by which he had been standing. 'It's as if we had a sort of telepathic communication between us.' Vicky, flushed by her strenuous ride and with her hair flying in the breeze, looked the picture of health, and her husband, his grey eyes flickering strangely, merely smiled at this and, possessing himself of her hand, walked along the fence, he on the outside, until they reached the gate. Cutey was left in the paddock to enjoy her rest and crop the lush green grass while Vicky and Richard strolled towards the house. It was as they were crossing the lawn that Richard said, his voice devoid of expression,

'Have you been over to see your father today?'

Vicky shook her head.

'No; I thought of going over for an hour or so before dinner.' Richard said nothing and she added, faintly puzzled, 'Is there any reason why you asked?'

He slanted her a glance, an unfathomable glance, as if he were debating something of vital importance. When presently he spoke Vicky detected a hint of guardedness in his tone.

'I saw him earlier on, when I was over in the woods that adjoin his land. He didn't look to be quite himself. Not so——'

'He didn't?' broke in Vicky, her heart jumping into her mouth. 'What was wrong with him?'

'He's not ill, my dear so there's no need for anxiety. It's just that he seemed to be a little pale, that's all.'

She looked up at his set profile and read nothing. Yet she sensed a certain anxiety about him not unmingled with regret. Fearfully she allowed her mind to dwell on the fact that two of her father's business friends had died of coronary thrombosis, one aged fifty-two and the other fifty-eight.

'I must go to him,' she faltered, 'at once!'

But Richard shook his head, tightening his grip on her hand in case she should think of running off immediately.

'We'll both go, Vicky, when you've washed and changed.'

She tugged at her hand, but to no avail.

'How was he when you spoke to him?' she wanted to know.

'Just as usual, darling. Jovial, talking about the new orchids which have been produced by his gardener.' Richard was watching the Labrador as he raced ahead. The dog had been with him by the fence and had walked sedately beside him and Vicky up till a few moments ago when he had begun romping over the lawn.

'Richard,' she said imploringly, 'I must go over, just to ease my mind.'

He frowned as if angry with himself.

'Perhaps I shouldn't have mentioned it,' he began.

'You did, though, because, if anything should happen, you didn't want me to have too great a shock—No, don't try to put me off, Richard. I sensed that you were guarded, as if you weren't very happy about telling me of your suspicions.'

'Darling, you're making a mountain out of a molehill! Your father might be off colour, but he's certainly not dangerously ill—as you're convincing yourself he is.'

'I want to go to him, now!'

'I'll drive you over—Vicky, come back!' But she had managed to break away from him and she fled towards the gate at the end of the shrubbery, her heart thudding painfully against her ribs. If anything should happen to her father! If he should be robbed of the rewards of his years of hard work.

'I couldn't bear it!' she cried, running on without even looking back. A sadness had come over her that had nothing to do with her father, a sadness that Richard was not with her, driving her to her father as he had suggested.

But she did not want Richard. How could she look for comfort to a husband whose only interest in her was the money he had procured for allowing her the honour of using his name?

Breathless when she arrived at the bungalow, Vicky tried to control her breathing, tried to assume a calmness of mien and bring a smile to her lips. Wallace was in the sitting-room, working at a low table, a file on the chair beside him, a glass of milk on the floor at his side.

'Vicky!' he greeted her, half in welcome and half in surprise. 'I didn't expect you at this time. I rather thought you and Richard might stroll over later, though, either before or after dinner. You've been riding, I see. How is Cutey?'

'Fine,' she replied absently, her eyes searching his face. 'Are you all right, Father?'

'All right? Of course I'm all right. What made you ask a question like that?' Reaching down, he lifted the glass. She watched him as he took a long drink of the milk.

'Richard said you were pale, this morning, when he was speaking to you.'

'And you came chasing over to see me?' His eyes with their absurd brows protruding over them slid over her slender body. 'Yes, you're not your immaculate self, I see. You had no need to panic simply because I was pale.' His mouth seemed to tighten in a way Vicky had never noticed before. 'Richard had no right to mention it. What exactly did he say to you?' he added almost angrily.

'Nothing to alarm me, really. I just had to come over, that's all.'

'Well, I'm fine, I assure you of that.' He put down the empty glass, which Vicky automatically picked up, holding it in her hand.

'I must admit you look all right, Father.' Her nerves having settled, Vicky was able to produce one of her bright smiles. 'What are you doing?'

'The accounts. I've definitely decided to retire.'

'I'm glad, in a way; it'll give you more time to enjoy yourself.' She sat down on a low chair which was in reality a 'sample' of the Regency period, French and exquisitely inlaid with mother-of-pearl in the back and the arms. Vicky had often wondered what those apprentices of far-off days would have thought could they have known how valuable their work would become. Carefully executed, the work-piece had been handed to the master craftsman who, after judging the article, would then decide the young apprentice's fate by giving his expert opinion of the work. 'What worries me, though,' went on Vicky, 'is that you might find life a little boring after all those years of activity.'

'I don't believe I shall, my dear. This house and garden are a delight to me, and I have you close——' His eyes wandered fleetingly over her. 'And who knows, I might—in the not-too-distant future—have my grandchildren coming over to sit on my knee and listen to my stories. Do you remember how you used to like to hear them?'

She was blushing, naturally, and he laughed, not bothering to wait for an answer as he went on to say that she must not keep him waiting for the news if—and when—she found herself like *that*.

Strange, she mused, but the idea had never even occurred to her. She supposed it would have done eventually ... but now she had no wish for Richard's children ...

No wish ... But children would come, unless ...

A sudden chill broke over her, but soon passed. She was practical all at once, making a re-assessment of her situation. Recently, the vacuum into which she had fallen was not so effective as at first, since no longer was the numbness of her mind able to shield her from pain. A sharp word from her husband was like a knife-thrust in her heart; his lovemaking seemed lustful—though she had to own that this might be imagination, born of the knowledge that he had no love for her. Her own responses seemed sordid to her, yet she could not control the desires which created them.

For her peace of mind, for the removal of the cause of her humiliation, there was only one step she could take: she must have that showdown with Richard.

And the opportunity came sooner than she expected; it came that very night when Richard, coming to her as she stood by the window, looking down into the moonlit garden, told her that he had forgotten to mention that he would be away for the whole of the next day, not returning until very late at night. Vicky, turning slowly, felt a sudden rise of anger at the calm and casual manner in which he said this. He was going to leave her all day ... but for now, he intended to enjoy the pleasure of her body!

She said, having rehearsed her part well and having determined that her father was not to suffer over this,

'I have something to discuss with you, Richard, but first I want your solemn promise that my father shall remain in total ignorance of what we're going to talk about.' She marvelled at her own composure, that although her heart was beating a little too quickly, it had no disturbing effect upon her.

Richard, clearly taken aback, stared interrogatingly at her, his mouth a little tight, as if he were tensed in some way.

'You want a promise from me? I don't quite know what you mean, Vicky.'

She slid her eyes over his long, slim body, clad in a

dressing-gown of green with red dragons printed upon it.

'I'm sure I made myself clear, Richard,' she said quietly, returning her eyes to his face. 'You and I have to discuss something—something serious. But I don't want my father to know about it, not ever. You said he was looking off colour this morning and although there seemed to be nothing wrong with him when I went over, I have reason to believe that he might not be feeling himself.'

Her husband's eyes flickered for a moment.

'You know that he's retiring, obviously.'

'I didn't think you would know,' she said, surprised.

'He told me.' Richard paused a moment as if unsure of what to say next. 'This discussion, Vicky . . . ?'

'Is about us—you and me. But first, the promise. It's important, Richard.'

'I give it,' he returned, his grey eyes fixed on hers. He seemed tensed and Vicky wondered if he had some idea of what she was about to say.

'Thank you.' Her voice was low, her eyes bright although she was very far from tears. They would come later, when the reaction set in.

'I know about the business arrangement you made with my father over our marriage.'

Silence, broken only by the slow, heavy tick of the antique clock on the wall. Richard's face was like a mask, stiff, unmoving. Vicky, though calm outside, felt that her heart was beating so loudly that Richard must be able to hear it.

'How did you find out about it?' Richard's voice broke into the silence, quietly, unemotionally, and it was only the hint of greyness at the sides of his mouth that gave any indication that he might not be feeling as composed as he seemed.

'You don't deny it?'

He shook his head.

'No, Vicky, I don't—I can't.'

'Because it's true?' Only now did she realise that she had, deep within her subconscious, been willing it to be untrue, been ready and eager to grasp at any explanation her husband might have to offer.

'Yes, it's true, but ...' He moved restlessly, knotting the tie of his dressing-gown which, when he entered, had been hanging loose. 'How did you find out?' he repeated without finishing the first sentence.

'I was in Buxton ...' Vicky went on to explain how she had met John Bailey, then, later, how she had overheard his colleague saying that Richard had married money. She stopped at that point as Richard, his composure deserting him for a moment, lifted a hand as if he would order her to go no further with her story.

'I can only say how sorry I am that this knowledge came to you in the way it did,' he said, his voice edged with a huskiness she had never heard in it before. 'There's much more to it than appears on the surface, but I could never hope to convince you that ...'

'My father did pay all your debts?' cut in Vicky in a stiff little voice.

Richard's teeth came together.

'Yes,' he answered tautly, 'he did.'

Again she looked at him, seeing no humility, but certainly regret. She said, wondering how she could voice the words so calmly,

'At the time my father first hinted to you that he'd like you to marry me—by this I mean when the proposition was first put to you—did you care for Louisa Austin?'

Richard turned, to stare through the window into the starry darkness of the mysterious moorlands in the distance.

'Yes,' he admitted at last, 'I did care for her at that time.'

Vicky felt as if all the power had left her body, all strength gone from her legs. She had known it, of course, but to hear her husband actually admit that he was in love with another girl was like the point of a sword in her heart.

In love with one girl but marrying another . . .

'Surely,' she said, 'she was upset?'

Richard turned, his brow furrowed, his grey eyes perplexed.

'You're so cool about it,' he began. 'Vicky, my dear——'

'Don't call me your dear! Not ever again! Calm, you say! Calm——' She laughed, hysteria very near to taking possession of her. 'How much did my father pay you for your giving me the honour to bear your illustrious name?'

'Vicky——'

'Answer me! How much?'

'That,' he replied, his voice taking on an edge of hardness, 'is a question I shall *not* answer.'

'I can guess. It must have been half of his capital.'

Richard made no comment, nor did his unmoving countenance convey any sign that she had come close to the truth, or that she was well out in her estimation. 'I must admit,' she said, her voice resuming its former quiet intonation, 'that you've managed very cleverly to deceive me. Did my father extract a promise from you that you'd never let me discover that you didn't love me?'

'Vicky,' he said, ignoring her question, 'there is, as I've said, much more to this than you're aware of—No, don't interrupt,' he said sternly when she opened her mouth to speak. 'I'm not going to try to vindicate myself in any way. I knew what I was doing. But——' he stopped, fixing her lovely eyes as if to command her to prepare

her mind to receive and absorb what he was about to
say next, '*there is more* than just the sordid arrangement
I made with your father——'

'There can't be!' she flashed, uncaring that he frowned
darkly at her for the interruption. 'And I'm glad you
called it sordid! What kind of man are you—loving one
girl and marrying another! I hate you—*hate you*, and I
always shall!'

He shook his head in protest.

'No! You can't hate me! I don't believe——'

'Why should you care anyway? You've got the money,
which is all you're interested in. I had intended to stay
with you, because of Father, and that's why I've kept it
to myself so long——'

'Kept it to yourself?' broke in Richard. 'How long
have you known?'

She told him, watching the deepening of the frown on
his forehead.

'It would appear that you're very good at acting.'

She looked away.

'It was for Father,' she began.

He seemed about to comment, but changed his mind,
referring to what she had said earlier.

'You say you *intended* to stay with me. Does this mean
that you're no longer going to?'

She hesitated, aware that her thoughts were far from
clear on that matter.

'I haven't had time to decide about my future ...' Her
voice faltered, but he did not appear to notice as he said,

'You kept this knowledge to yourself for three weeks;
why then have you decided to tell me now?' So cool the
tone! But, glancing at his grim set profile, Vicky noticed
a nerve in his throat. It pulsated all the time, betraying
an emotional disturbance within him.

'Originally, I had believed I must—and could—keep

what I'd learned to myself. I was afraid of upsetting Father. But I changed my mind, realising I could get the promise from you.' She stopped, but it was plain to him that she had not completed what she should have said in answer to his question, and so he prompted her, but even then he had to wait some moments before he heard her say, through lips that seemed scarcely to move. 'I didn't want to find myself carrying a child of yours ...'

A terrible silence fell between them, heavy, pressing, like the hush of doom. Vicky was amazed that Richard could lose so much of his colour.

'I see ...' he managed at last, though his voice was little more than a whisper. 'So I'm to take it that the intimate side of our marriage is ended?'

For one wild moment of yearning Vicky could have flung herself into his arms, had him kiss away the agony that was tearing at her heart. Instead she lifted her head, sent him a look of spurning disdain and said yes, he was correct in his assumption that the intimate side of their marriage was ended. And she added that if it was not for her father, and the fear of hurting him, the marriage would be ended altogether.

Richard seemed weighed down, and for a time he could find nothing to say, but in a little while his voice came to her, low, distressed, and filled with a bitter regret that escaped his wife altogether.

'Vicky dear, I'm sorry, so very sorry——'

'Don't!' she cried, eyes blazing. 'Sorry! What sort of a word is that to express contrition for what you've done to me?'

'Whatever I do or say will be equally futile,' he admitted. 'I can only try again to tell you that you don't know the whole of this. One day I might be able ...' He allowed his voice to fade, his shoulders sagging in a gesture of utter hopelessness and despair.

'I'm not interested in any excuses you might try to concoct in order to hoodwink me again!' Vicky was quivering with anger, seeing his attitude as one of near indifference, so little emotion was showing in his face. He said nothing and she added, her temper subsiding again, 'You made a promise. Nothing of this must get back to my father.'

'I'm a man of my word, Vicky.'

'I hope so, though it amazes me that you are.'

Ignoring this, he said quietly,

'You're furiously angry with me, which is understandable, but you're not angry with your father, apparently?'

'I've forgiven him. He's happy that his ambition— that of seeing me married to a man of some consequence —has been realised. I've no wish to rob him of that happiness, especially as he's not too well.'

'You've forgiven him, but you won't ever forgive me?'

'I shall neither forgive you, nor forget, for one moment of the day, what you've done to me.' She looked at him across the room. 'I hadn't done anything to deserve that you'd treat me so wickedly, so cruelly——'

'Vicky, my dear,' he broke in, taking a step towards her, 'I know how you feel, how deeply you're hurt. Your father told me that you were in love with me——'

'I was in love with you,' she interrupted, having to make a desperate attempt to keep the anguish from her voice, 'but I'm not in love with you now.'

The hush that fell on the room was beyond the interruption of words. Vicky was to recall it many times ... recall it but fail to understand it, just as she failed to understand it now. Nor did she understand why Richard's face had blanched, why he seemed to sway a little, as she herself had done a moment or two ago. Her eyes, misted but tearless, strayed to his hands; they were so tightly clenched that it almost seemed that the knuckles would break through the whitened skin.

'I can't say anything more tonight, Vicky,' he said at last in tones of weariness. 'Goodnight, my dear ...' His voice tailed off; he turned on his heel and the next moment Vicky was standing there, by the great four-poster bed, staring at the closed door.

This was what she wanted; this was the reason why she had decided on the showdown. She closed her eyes tightly, but her tears escaped, flooding her cheeks and falling on to the front of her dainty négligé, wetting it through. At last she got into bed and snapped off the light. She wondered if she would sleep, wondered if she would ever sleep again.

The following day she rose with a weight on her heart so heavy that every movement seemed too much for her. Unable to eat her breakfast she wandered about the garden, Kaliph at her heels. Lunch was merely a nibble or two at the food put before her and then she went off again, wanting to go to her father but quite convinced that he would take one look at her and demand to know what was wrong. At last she decided to go on to the moors, was disappointed in not being able to find the dog, and went alone, where she roamed all the afternoon and into the evening, trying to think, to see a way, a glimmer of light that would brighten her life. But there was only a wall of darkness before her, a wall she knew she would never be able to scale. The sheer magnitude of the bleakness facing her was terrifying—years and years, and more years of existing while those around her lived and loved and laughed.

She thought of the past, those happy years of contentment and peace of mind, and she wondered dismally what she was gaining by her reflections.

The evening shadows began to fall and she realised she was still a long way from the Manor. Turning, she decided to cut across country, since she had no desire to be out here on the lonely moors after dark. Not that there would be anyone to harm her—Vicky's thoughts were cut abruptly and her heart jerked as in the near distance a figure loomed, emerging from behind a little bluff in the hillside. A man! Her instinct was to run, but the man was in her path. To run the other way would not gain her anything as it merely took her further into the grim moorlands.

Trying to still her palpitation she decided to go on, walking quickly as if she were not afraid of anything. The low hills that formed part of the moorlands were taking on a dun sort of colour, their sides cast into shadows as the sun's last rays disappeared below the horizon. Vicky glanced swiftly around her, fear welling up in spite of her outward calm as she continued her brisk pace. Then she saw who it was and a great wave of relief swept through her. John Bailey! But what was he doing here, on the lonely moors, at this time of the day?

'Mrs Sherrand!' He stopped even before he reached her. 'My, but am I relieved to see you! I'm hopelessly lost!'

'Lost?' blinked Vicky, glancing around. 'How do you come to be here anyway?'

'Surveying the old lady's land.' He automatically tapped the large pasteboard folder he carried under his arm. 'I left the car near an old quarry——' He swung a hand vaguely. 'It's in a little clearing right off the road. I expect you know where I mean?'

Vicky shook her head, explaining that the area was riddled both with disused quarries and coalmines.

'Have you no idea which way you've come?' she added,

wrinkling her brow in concentration. 'There's an over-grown quarry on the Wyevale road.'

'Where's that?'

'It's some distance from here, I'm afraid.'

'I've been walking for almost an hour and a half—wandering around in circles from what I can make out.' His voice was strained, his manner anxious. 'I hope the car's all right.'

'It will be,' returned Vicky reassuringly. 'I don't suppose anyone's been past it, even.'

'What a deserted no-man's land this is,' he complained. 'I'm not sure at all that I'll recommend it for building.'

'I told you it was wild moorland. It's fit only for sheep rearing.'

'Which way is the Manor?' he asked. 'If I can come with you—You are going home, I presume?'

She nodded.

'Yes. And of course you can come with me. I'll get my car out and drive around with you until you find yours.'

'That's kind of you,' he said gratefully.

'Didn't you bring your map?' she inquired as the thought occurred to her.

'A map's not much good to you if you can't pinpoint where you are,' he said with a laugh.

'No, of course not.' She glanced around, noting that apart from the few low hills, there was nothing but featureless terrain totally devoid of landmarks.

They began to stride out, Vicky feeling thankful that she had company since the dusk was falling rather more quickly than usual, aided by some low clouds that were gathering darkly over the moors.

'What a lucky thing I met you,' John Bailey was saying. 'I'd have been here all night once darkness had fallen.' He paused as if considering whether or not he should question the 'lady of the manor'. However, her extreme youth gave him courage and he asked how she came to be out here, all alone, so late in the day.

'I felt like a long walk,' she replied.

'It's a wonder your husband would let you come.' Another hesitation and then, 'It must be past your dinner-time, surely?'

'My husband's not at home, so I shan't bother about dinner.' Even as she spoke an idea came to her. 'How long is it since you ate?' she asked, and her companion gave a grimace as he answered,

'Just about eight hours! I had an early lunch before leaving Manchester, thinking I'd call at an hotel on the way back. But they'll all have finished serving dinner by the time I reach civilisation.'

Vicky remained silent for a while, thoughtfully going over her idea. Would Richard approve of her bringing a strange young man home to dinner? Did it matter whether he approved or not? She wasn't asking him to join them in the meal; he wouldn't be there anyway, as he'd said he would be home very late.

'You can have dinner with me if you like,' she suggested at last.

'That's generous of you! But you said you weren't having any,' he reminded her.

'I *can* have some, though.' She paused, wondering why she was so anxious to have this young man's company. She had felt so lonely all day, so perhaps any human being would have been welcome at this time. 'Cook will be able to get something ready in half an hour or so.'

'Well, I do thank you. To tell you the truth, I'm absolutely starving!'

'I should think so, having nothing in all that time. If you prefer it we can eat before we go for your car?'

He shook his head and said, hungry though he was,

he'd feel far more comfortable when he had collected the car.

'It's my own this time, you see,' he explained with a rueful grin, 'so I'm rather more anxious than I'd be if it was the firm's.'

'We'll go and hunt around for the car, then,' she said, increasing her pace a little. 'I think we ought to hurry; it looks as if it's going to rain.'

'Yes, you're right.'

They strode out even faster, Vicky trotting now and then to keep pace with him. He turned several times to slant her a glance of admiration. And after a while he ventured to say that she was not the kind of girl he would have expected so exalted a man as Richard Sherrand to have for a wife.

'I don't mean anything—— Oh, dear, I'm afraid I'm not always diplomatic,' he apologised ruefully.

'You think I'm too young?' Vicky had the niggling thought that this was wrong; as the wife of Richard Sherrand she should by rights possess that kind of dignity that would set her above a conversation of this kind. But as she herself had so many times admitted, she was not of the same social level as her husband. In any case, John Bailey knew that Richard had 'married money', so it was no use pretending to be what she was not. John was a highly intelligent young man and it was feasible to assume that he was drawing his own conclusions as to why she, a comparatively new bride, was on her own like this. There was no love in the marriage, he would be thinking.

'Yes, I suppose it is your youth,' John was saying. 'Also, you're so—friendly.'

'I'm a Lancashire lass; we don't seem to be able to cultivate much reserve.'

'I'm from Lancashire myself.' He cast her the kind of

glance that said, 'So we're comrades; that's great!'

Vicky in her desperately unhappy state was ready to receive the spontaneous friendliness which her companion
extended to her. In the bleak dark recesses of her mind
lurked the knowledge that her marriage was finished in
all but name, her life in consequence held nothing. This
young man walking beside her needed only the barest
amount of encouragement to be her friend ...

They reached the Manor at last, and the rain had kept
off. Vicky, after telling cook to prepare a quick meal
which could be eaten in about half an hour's time, took
her car from the garage and drove John along the roads
which she thought might lead eventually to their spotting
his car. The dusk gave way to night; the clouds cleared
miraculously and the moon appeared.

'Well, that's going to be a help,' commented John with
relief. 'The car's a darkish blue and I was beginning to
wonder if we'd miss it in the darkness.' He was scanning
one side of the road and Vicky the other. They travelled
for mile after mile, not leaving any lane unexamined, no
matter how small and narrow it might be. At last John
gave a sharp exclamation and she drew in to the side.
'Thank goodness! I was beginning to wonder if we were
going to drive around like this until midnight!'

A quarter of an hour later they were back at the
Manor, with Cook not appearing too pleased at having to
keep the meal warm. She cast a curious glance at John before saying,

'You said to have it ready in half an hour, madam.
That's almost an hour ago.'

'I'm sorry,' murmured Vicky. 'Please serve the dinner
now.'

'Very good, madam.' Another glance at John and she
was gone.

John turned his attention from the cook's disappearing

back and looked at Vicky. She coloured, embarrassed at having to apologise to the servant in front of John. He said forthrightly, seeming to be quite disproportionately angry,

'I can't say I care for her! If she were my employee I'd have given her a darned good telling off.'

Vicky bit her lip, aware that the tears were close.

'I don't take any notice,' she said. 'Would you like to wash your hands? If so, the cloakroom's just there—the second door on the right.'

He went off and she waited until he joined her again, taking him into the drawing-room and giving him a drink before going off herself to wash her hands and face and tidy her hair. She did not change as she would have done had she been dining with Richard, but when she joined her visitor she saw his eyes flicker as he gave her an appraising glance.

'May I say how very pretty you are, Mrs Sherrand?'

A silence followed, strange and intimate. Vicky felt she would burst into tears if he became too friendly, too kind to her. She said quietly,

'Thank you, Mr Bailey. Er—if you've finished your drink we'll go into the other room.'

He followed her; she indicated a chair, but he pulled hers out first. The soup was brought in, then the second course of fried chicken, mushrooms and french fried potatoes. John tucked in, apologising as he helped himself to more chicken, which was in a covered dish over a spirit stove.

'Don't apologise,' said Vicky. 'You must be ravenous.'

'I was, but already I'm feeling better. You're most kind,' he said. 'I don't know how to thank you.'

'There's no need for thanks. Inviting you to dinner was the only practical thing to do.'

His big frank eyes settled on her face.

'Are you often practical?' he wanted to know, and Vicky could not help wondering if he were thinking about her marriage. He would not know, of course, that she had been hoodwinked; on the contrary, he must have concluded that she had not minded being married for her money. She was now the mistress of this lovely stately home and he would obviously think that this was what she had aimed for. She frowned, hating the idea that John should think such things about her, yet she had no way of disillusioning him other than by telling him the truth, which quite naturally she was not willing to do.

'My father was a practical man,' she told John in answer to his question, 'and I take after him.'

'Your father? Does he live around these parts?'

For a fleeting moment she hesitated and then,

'He lives at the bungalow on the other side of the hill.'

'The bungalow——?' Pohn stopped eating, his fork poised above his plate, his expression almost comical in its concern. 'Lord, I made a *faux pas* that first day, then?'

She smiled, faintly surprised that she could actually have laughed.

'Yes, you did, rather.'

'Why didn't you tell me it was your father's bungalow?'

Vicky shrugged indifferently.

'It didn't matter.'

'But it did,' he protested. 'I'm never deliberately tactless.'

'And you weren't deliberately tactless at that time,' she pointed out, her eyes on his plate. 'There's fruit and cream for the sweet, or you can have gateau if you feel you still need something more substantial.'

'By that you mean filling,' he grinned. 'Yes, please, I'll have the gateau.' He was quite at home already, noticed Vicky, amazed to discover that the tensions within her had been released, that she had actually enjoyed her meal, though on sitting down at the table she had not been in the least hungry. 'What are you having?' John was asking her as the gateau appeared.

Vicky said she would have a little of the fruit, but she sat and finished her wine first. She was fully aware of her companion's interest, his admiring stare, though she could not of course know exactly what he was seeing—the arch of her throat beneath the pointed little chin, the rosy mouth, the serious eyes with their frame of long dark lashes, the clear wide forehead beneath the gleaming hair, hair stranded with burnished gold and falling so naturally into its style of the page-boy bob. He glanced down suddenly, as if he would now hide his expression from her.

Twenty minutes later he was glancing at the clock in the hall, ruefully estimating how long it would take him to get home.

'I had no idea it was so late,' Vicky had said a moment previously. 'A quarter to twelve!'

'We were such a long time finding the car,' he reminded her. 'And in addition we'd done an hour or more's hike over those moors.'

She nodded.

'Yes, and it was already beginning to get dark. Well, I hope you have a safe journey home ...' Her voice trailed off as she heard a car crunch to a halt on the forecourt. 'My husband,' she elucidated, though she rather thought this was unnecessary. 'I'm wondering if you ought to stay the night. It's so very late and you must be tired. Shall I ask my husband if he minds?'

'Well ...' It was clear that John wanted to stay ... and Vicky wanted him to stay. 'If you think——' He broke off as the front door swung inwards. Vicky, pale but composed, immediately explained what had happened, first reminding Richard that he knew John—or at least, he knew of him.

'Yes, we have met,' said both men together, then fell silent as Vicky continued with her explanation. She ended up by suggesting that John should stay the night. To her surprise Richard hesitated, a frown crossing his face. As John had suddenly discovered that his shoelace was undone, and stooped to tie it, he missed both Richard's hesitation and his frown. Vicky, acutely aware that the idea of John's staying did not please him in the least, lifted her chin and looked directly into his eyes, the martial expression in her own plainly being a challenge.

'Yes,' murmured Richard then, 'it will be all right for Mr Bailey to stay.'

'Thank you, Mr Sherrand,' returned John, deliberately keeping his eyes off Vicky. 'That's most kind of you. I must say, I wasn't looking forward to driving to Manchester at this time of the night. There's such a lot of moorland to cross before you get to any really good roads.'

Later, when Vicky was in her bedroom, clad only in a diaphanous nightgown, as she was about to get into bed, Richard knocked quietly, then entered without waiting for her to speak.

'How did you come to be on the moors in the dark?' he demanded almost harshly.

'It wasn't dark,' returned Vicky briefly.

He looked at her, his eyes seeming to strip the flimsy covering from her altogether. She sensed a smouldering fury beneath the cold unsmiling scrutiny to which he was subjecting her.

'How long were you out there?'

'All the afternoon——'

'All——!' His mouth tightened. 'It's far too lonely out there for a woman on her own!'

Vicky's eyes held nothing but contempt.

'Why should you be so concerned? It isn't as though you really care what happens to me.'

A silence fell on the room for a space before Richard said, the control of his voice such that she wondered now if she had imagined that anger of a few seconds ago.

'In spite of any conclusions you might have come to, Vicky, I do care what happens to you. You're my wife——'

'The wife whose death would make you even richer than you are now, simply because Father has settled money on me, so if I'd been murdered out there on the moors——'

'Shut up!' he snarled, taking a step towards her. 'I'm not interested in any money you might leave!'

'Perhaps you have all you need. Just how much *did* my father pay you for marrying me?'

'Vicky,' warned Richard, taking another step forward, 'I'm in no mood to take your insults meekly, or even calmly.'

'What's wrong?' she asked, driven by some force she could not control. 'Did you have a quarrel with Louisa?'

'I haven't seen Louisa!'

The contempt appeared in her expression again.

'That I can't believe. You've admitted you're in love with her——' Vicky stopped, brought to a halt by the sudden start he gave. 'You *have* admitted it,' she said again, endeavouring to read his expression. 'And so it's feasible that you're with her on these occasions when you're supposed to be meeting business associates.' Her tone had risen slightly to include a scoffing note, which, she soon realised, inflamed her husband, for tiny threads of crimson began to creep up the sides of his mouth, the colour causing drifts beneath the tan of his skin.

'Be careful,' he advised. 'I've been gentle with you up till now, Vicky, but there's a side to me which, if ever you see it, is going to surprise you.'

She said nothing for the moment. What he said was true, she decided, recalling those times when he had seemed so formidable to her, with those harsh lines about his face and a mouth that was far too thin. She knew now that this side of him had been in evidence owing to the strain he had been going through at that time, with debts pressing on him, his stepmother's probable demands, his home in danger of coming under the auctioneer's hammer. Yes, that harsh formidable countenance was the outward sign of the 'side' of which he had just spoken. She looked at him now, saw that his features had relaxed, and her heart caught so that the pain was almost physical. How attractive he was! And how she wanted him to take her in his arms, to kiss her in that possessive way, to pick her up and carry her to—Vicky cut her thoughts abruptly, anger filling her at the thought of his making love to her without love. He was speaking again, asking to hear more about her afternoon on the moors.

'There's nothing to tell,' she answered mechanically. 'It started to get dark and I was making my way back when I met——'

'You've already told me that,' he broke in, but gently. 'Vicky, why were you out there at all, roaming about on your own? You must have been there for several hours. Was the dog with you?'

She shook her head, wishing he would go, because the tears were far too close.

'No, I couldn't find him; he'd gone off somewhere.'

Richard seemed to give a deep sigh.

'You mustn't ever go off like that again,' he said. 'Will you promise me you won't?'

She lifted her chin and said outright,

'No, I won't make any promises to you at all. I shall do exactly as I like.'

The grey eyes kindled, and narrowed to mere slits.

'By God, you won't do exactly as you like! You'll do as I tell you! And I'm telling you not to roam over those moors again. Understand?' He was close now, tall and overpowering and menacing. Vicky felt her heartbeats increase as fear swept over her. She had no intention of obeying the order he had just given, but nevertheless she was not prepared to prolong this situation. And so she replied, with a meekness which she knew would satisfy him,

'Yes, Richard, I understand.'

'Wise girl!' he said, and swinging round on his heel he left the room, closing the central door with rather more noise than was necessary.

CHAPTER EIGHT

THE following morning Vicky was up early, but John Bailey was before her. She saw him from the morning-room window as she looked out on to the garden. Quite naturally she went out to him, managing to produce a smile in response to his.

'I didn't think last night,' she began after they had greeted one another, 'but you would have wanted to telephone your people, saying you wouldn't be home.'

'I live alone, in a flat,' he told her. 'It's a nice way to be; you haven't to answer to anyone.' Vicky said nothing to this and John went on, 'I'd like to be on my way by about nine o'clock, although I shall be coming back the day after tomorrow to see the old lady who's selling the land.'

'The moorlands? You didn't think they were of any value, you said.'

'She has a great deal of land besides that. We're definitely interested in some land she owns near Wellsover.' John looked at her, taking in the pale skin, the mouth that was faintly sad, the shadow in her eyes. 'When I come back,' he ventured, 'can I see you?'

Her eyes flickered; she began to shake her head, then changed her mind.

'I don't understand what you mean,' she murmured at length.

'I think you do ... Vicky.'

She swallowed; he was moving too fast for her.

'How did you know my name?' she asked, playing for time. They were standing by the shrubbery, but Vicky began to walk on, aware that if Richard should happen to be looking through his bedroom window he must see them. A little arbour offered shelter and it was towards this that she was making her way, John setting his pace to hers.

'I heard your husband use it last night.'

'Of course; I'd forgotten.'

He said, after having some difficulty with his phrasing, 'You're not happy, are you?'

'Is it so plain for everyone to see?' The words were out before she realised it.

'Yes, Vicky, it is.'

'Of course, you know that my husband——' She broke off, appalled that she could have been going to talk about Richard's perfidy.

'Married you for your money, yes,' came the quiet voice of the man beside her. 'But how did you know that I knew that?'

Vicky swallowed again; her throat seeming to have gone dry. It was so humiliating to talk about such things as being married for what she could bring as a dowry, but after a moment of thought she decided that as John knew so much there was little point in her stopping now. Besides, his interest was like balm to her pain. She *wanted* to talk to someone and it seemed providential that he had appeared at this time.

'I happened to overhear your colleague, Danny, telling you that he'd discovered how my husband happened to come into the money which enabled him to withdraw his land,' she told him, her pensive gaze fixed on the entrance to the arbour as she and John approached it.

'You——' John turned his head, deep distress in his voice as he continued, 'How the devil did that come about? Oh, what a dreadful thing to overhear! Did you hear it *all*?'

Vicky said no, she hadn't heard it all, as they walked away. But she had heard the beginning of what Danny was saying.

'I was standing looking in a shop window when this friend came up to you and said——' Vicky shook her head, saying it did not matter. 'Shall we go and have breakfast?' She suggested then, making to turn and re-trace her steps. John took her arm and pushed her gently through the little archway that formed the entrance to the arbour.

'In a few minutes.' Once inside, with no fear of their being seen, he took her hand in his, surprised that she made no attempt to snatch it away—but not so surprised as Vicky herself. 'I'm so sorry,' he said in a troubled tone. 'What a harrowing experience for you. I wish I'd known you were so close.'

'You couldn't have done anything, John. Your friend spoke so quickly that you couldn't have stopped him in time.'

He was looking at her strangely, and she waited, puzzled by his silence.

'Do you realise, Vicky, that you called me John?'

She looked a trifle bewildered.

'Did I?' she said without a trace of embarrassment.

'Yes, and it came out so naturally that anyone would conclude you'd been doing it for some time ... that we were friends, in fact.' A question in this, and once again Vicky felt he was moving too fast for her. Yet she needed him, there was no doubt in her mind about that. She could not confide in her father; she had no brothers or sisters, no friends even. Yes, she needed him, and if he wanted to be her friend then she was grateful for that friendship. 'Vicky ...' His voice drifted to her, but she kept her face averted. 'Are we to be friends, dear?'

She nodded, still without looking up.

'I'd like that, John,' she answered simply. She looked at his hand, holding hers. It resembled her father's hands—rather plump but warm and comforting. Not like Richard's hands, long and lean and strong ... hands which she knew instinctively could hurt.

'So we can meet when I return the day after to-morrow?'

'Yes, if—if you like.'

'You're so attractive, Vicky, that I can't understand your husband at all. Even if he didn't marry you for love, it's a miracle to me that he hasn't fallen in love with you since.'

'He loves another girl.' Vicky marvelled at the coldly objective way she could handle this conversation. There was no emotion in her voice, no pain within her heart. She could only conclude that even yet again she had become mercifully enfolded in that vacuum which offered her relief from the anguish which should surely have over-whelmed her as she spoke of the girl her husband loved.

'Another girl?' John stared in disbelief. 'But—so soon——' He let go of her hand so that he could spread both of his. 'It's not possible! How long have you been married?'

'He was in love with her before we married.'

'Good God!' John's face had coloured with anger. 'Vicky, you can't mean that he loved one girl but married another—just for her money?'

'This girl's father appears to be in financial difficulties, so he couldn't give Richard any money.' Vicky stopped, her lip quivering. 'I don't want to talk about it any more, John,' she said in choked accents.

He frowned to himself.

'Vicky, can I ask you a question?'

'I think I know what it is, and the answer's yes, I do love him.'

Silence, long and profound.

'I thought you might have made a bargain but now that I know you a little better I realise you wouldn't ever marry unless it was for love. You poor child!' He would have taken her in his arms but she moved away, saying it was time they went in as her husband would be sure to be up by now.

As it happened, he had been up at seven o'clock, ten minutes after his wife, and no sooner had John made his departure, having arranged to meet Vicky at Buxton the day after tomorrow, than Richard said, his voice taut with suppressed anger,

'How long were you out there with that fellow?'

'Until breakfast time. I'd have come in sooner if I'd known you were up. But I don't suppose you minded us not joining you for breakfast. You probably preferred to be alone.'

'Vicky, you know that's not true! You and I always have our breakfast together. I thought, when you didn't put in an appearance, that you weren't up. I had mine because I wanted to be in my office early. It was as I was looking out of my office window that I saw you strolling in the garden with Mr Bailey.' He noted her pallid face and a spasm of pain seemed to pass through him. 'I asked how long you were out there,' he reminded her.

'About half an hour.'

'I rather think it was longer, Vicky.'

'An hour, then. What does it matter?'

'Just what is this attitude you're intending to take?' he asked, his voice low and distressed.

'I've changed?' Vicky shrugged with feigned indifference. 'Naturally I have. I expect it doesn't please you that I'm no longer timid and tractable.'

'I didn't notice that you were timid, Vicky—just rather naïve and somewhat shy.' His voice had dropped almost to tenderness, but this was lost on his wife. 'I said last night that there's much more to the business of our marriage than appears on the surface, though for several reasons I'm finding difficulty in explaining.'

'I'm glad you referred to it as *business*,' Vicky could not resist retorting. 'As for the rest of what you've said, I'm not interested,' and with that she walked away, leaving him standing in the hall, a nerve throbbing in his throat, totally out of control.

She went to the paddock, saddled Cutey, then rode over to see her father before going on to the riding-club. Wallace was in his study; she knocked gently before entering. He looked up with a slight start from the paper that lay before him on his desk, and Vicky's heart gave a jerk as she noticed the grey tinge of his skin, the drawn mouth.

'Father ... are you all right?' she faltered, her thoughts flying quite naturally to that other occasion when she had come racing across after Richard had told her that Wallace was looking off colour. He had seemed all right, but as Vicky later told her husband, she did not think her father was in his usual perfect health. She had not been too anxious, though, since he was definitely not looking in any way *ill*. But now ... 'You don't look well at all, Father.'

'Don't look well?' he repeated, obviously attempting to bluff his way out of a situation for which he had not been prepared. 'What are you talking about, my precious? Of course I'm well. Have you ever known your old dad to be anything else?' He rose and came round the desk to plant a light kiss on her cheek. 'Are you off to the riding-club?'

'I don't think so, Father. I'm sending for the doctor.'

'Not on your life! I'm perfectly all right, my lamb, so just you stop all this nonsense!'

Vicky looked at his face again, her eyes dark with anxiety.

'Darling,' she said imploringly, 'please have the doctor.'

He moved impatiently, as if angry with himself.

'Why didn't you give me a ring to say you were coming? You always do—well, mostly you do.'

'I didn't think it was necessary at this time of the day. Besides, I wasn't intending to stay long.' Her keen gaze caused him to lower his eyelashes, which, he soon realised, only served to increase her anxiety. 'You wanted warning that I'd be coming over,' she said accusingly, 'and now you can't look at me. You're telling me a lie, Father, when you say you're feeling fine.'

He made no further denial, but looked into her anxious face and said,

'I'll admit I've been off colour, Vicky love, but it's not all that serious——'

'What do you mean by that?' she demanded, her eyes filling up. 'It's serious—but not too serious? Is that what you mean?'

He looked down at the carpet, one hand clenched tightly at his side.

'It's the old heart, love—Now,' he said sharply, wagging a finger at her, 'don't panic, or start to cry! You'll not be an orphan for donkeys' years yet. I've had the doctor and I'm taking pills. You can last for twenty years or more on pills these days. By jove, we're lucky to be living in these wonderful times when once fatal diseases are fatal no longer.'

Vicky listened, her heart beating wildly, for in spite

of what her father had been saying, she did see herself as an orphan, with no one in the whole world who loved her. But more impressive on her mind was the picture of her father, working, slaving, *grinding* his way through forty years of hard labour in order to realise an ambition conceived when he was little more than a child. And now that he could enjoy the fruits of that labour, he was dangerously ill. Bitterly she allowed her thoughts to dwell on the fact that the person who was really enjoying the fruits of that labour was her husband. How could she still be in love with him! It was infamous that she should be. He was a cheat, a mercenary cheat whose conscience never troubled him, who must secretly be laughing at Wallace, considering him the world's greatest fool to work like that only to give his money away. Not that Wallace had given it all away; but Vicky estimated that he had probably given Richard at *least* a quarter of his capital, but probably much more.

'So you had the doctor?' she heard herself murmuring. 'When was the first time you saw him?'

'About three months ago.'

'Three months!' She stared at him, her exclamation a rebuke. 'Father, how could you keep it from me?' Three months ... Just around the time that Richard had become interested in her ...

'Was there anything to be gained by not keeping it from you, my pet?'

'I don't know how you managed to see the doctor without my knowing. But it seems that you did. You haven't ever had an attack, have you?'

'No dear. It was the slightest pain at first, then a sort of breathlessness. I had a terrible fear of leaving you, my darling child—a terrible fear, as money's nothing if you haven't someone to love you, to take care of you. That's why I went to the doctor; I had to, had to make sure I didn't go until you were safely settled in life. Well, you are safely settled, and as for me—— I'm going to live for many years, as I've just said.'

Ignoring that part of his little speech which referred to her being safely settled, Vicky asked him if he had had it from the doctor that he would live for many years yet. He assured her that he had the doctor's word, going on to say that he would always have to take tablets, though.

'And you never forget to take them?'

'No, love, never.'

'Yet you were not well when I came into this room, were you?'

'I must admit that I was a little off colour, pet. But look at me now! It's gone and I'm ready for anything again.'

She did look at him, and was forced to agree with what he had said. Although she was still greatly troubled she was in some measure reassured, knowing that he spoke the truth when he said that people with a heart complaint could live for years if they took the tablets regularly. He would even be able to lead a normal life, but of course there would not be any heavy work. He was finished with that anyway.

'Is your health the reason why you've decided to retire?' she was asking presently, and he nodded at once.

'Yes, dear, I feel that it's time I gave it over to someone younger and more energetic.'

'Gave it over?' she repeated questioningly. 'I thought you were just—well, winding everything up, so to speak?'

To her surprise he made no comment on this; in fact, he changed the subject altogether, referring to the show that was to be held on the following Saturday.

'Are you all ready for it?' he asked, smiling affectionately at her. 'I shall be there, with your husband, expecting you to give a good account of yourself even if you don't win.'

'I don't know if I want to take part,' returned Vicky dejectedly.

'Because of me? Look here, Vicky, just you buck up! Richard won't be very pleased to see you looking like this.'

She turned away, wishing she could tell him everything. 'I'll enter,' she promised. 'But I don't think I shall win anything. Louisa might be competing, and it's said that she's a regular winner at all the shows.'

'Louisa?' he said sharply, frowning. 'Louisa Austin?'

'That's right.' Her tone was expressionless. 'She's been in hospital, though, so she might not be riding.'

His eyes flickered oddly.

'How do you know she's been in hospital?'

'I heard it somewhere,' she answered, adding quickly, 'Trudie was talking about her the other day. I've told you about Trudie, haven't I?'

'The friend you've made at the riding-club—yes, you have, love.'

She said after a pause,

'Shall I stay with you, Father?'

'I'm busy, dear,' he replied. 'I've such a lot to do, as you can imagine. Just you go and enjoy yourself over those jumps—but be careful, now! We don't want any broken bones!'

She agreed to leave him, but although she tried to throw off her fears she found it impossible. Always she recalled those two friends of his, dying so quickly of heart attacks.

However, once at the club she felt better. She more than satisfied everyone that she would put up a good show on Saturday, but she was again warned of the excellent championship results which Louisa Austin had acheived over the past few years.

'I didn't think she'd be riding,' Vicky heard Trudie say when they were in the snack bar drinking coffee. 'She's been in hospital, I've heard.'

'That's right, and apparently she shouldn't be riding. But she's a tough one, that, and has decided to ride after all.' This came from another young member of the club, Belinda Stowe, who was sitting on the stool next to Trudie. 'It's to be hoped she doesn't drive herself too hard, but if the competition's keen she certainly will drive herself, *and* the poor horse.'

Vicky listened to this, but it did not register too deeply. Little did she know that it was to register *very* deeply—on the day of the show.

When she got back to the Manor Richard was by the paddock, chatting with one of the gardeners. He turned, sliding his eyes over her as she rode up, then took the bridle from her as she swung lightly from the saddle.

'Did you have a good ride?' he asked, beginning to unsaddle the horse.

'Yes, thank you, Richard.' The gardener had wandered away but she spoke civilly, just in case her voice should carry. 'It was marvellous.'

'Do you think you'll have a chance of winning on Saturday?'

The gardener was now out of earshot, she noticed. He was making for the rear garden where the vegetable plots were.

'Your girl-friend's riding, so I don't expect I have a chance.'

Richard seemed to wince at her coldly-spoken words.

'Need you adopt that attitude, Vicky?' he began. 'I've

decided that we should talk, my dear.'

'If you think that you can exonerate yourself then you must think I'm a complete fool!'

'You're a fool if you don't listen to me.'

'I'd expect to hear nothing but lies.'

Richard's face paled a little, with anger.

'I warned you to take care, Vicky.'

'What more can you do to me?' she challenged.

The grey eyes darkened, dangerously.

'There are many things I could do to you,' he told her pointedly. 'At present I'm trying to be patient. In fact, it's not possible that I can be otherwise in certain matters. But with you, Vicky, I'm liable to lose my temper, and if I do then I shan't be responsible for my actions.'

'Are you threatening me with violence, Richard?' How cool and composed she was! But she had grown up all at once, and in addition she no longer felt inferior. In social status he might be on a higher level than she, but in uprightness and honesty of purpose he was very much lower.

'Don't be melodramatic!' chided Richard.

'Well, it seems to me that it's violence you're threatening me with. You speak of losing your temper . . .' She was talking to herself, for Richard, with a look of wrathful censure in his eyes, had turned from her and was striding away towards the house.

Dinner was a silent meal, as was to be expected, and Vicky went to bed without even saying goodnight to her husband. The next day she lunched with John in Buxton, at an hotel. When she arrived home it was almost dinner time, as she and John had driven into the hills of Derbyshire, taking a long time about it. He told her of the deal he was expecting to pull off with Louisa's aged aunt. The land near Wellsover was very valuable indeed and would fetch a small fortune when it was sold.

'Probably half a million,' went on John, 'because you know the value of land these days.'

Half a million, thought Vicky not without bitterness as she related this sum to her father's fortune. It had taken him almost thirty years to earn his first half a million, for the second half had come much more quickly than the first.

'You said that the money was to go to Miss Austin's niece or nephew. I don't think she had a nephew, only one niece, Louisa.' Vicky still marvelled at the way in which she could speak about the girl her husband loved.

'That's right. This girl's going to be wealthy.'

'How long does a deal like this take?'

'Could be a year, but if I have my way it'll go through in under six months.'

Richard was nowhere to be seen when Vicky returned, having picked up her car in Buxton where she had left it to go for the drive with John. She parked on the forecourt intending to go over to the bungalow later, when she had eaten. She went upstairs to bathe and change, and as she surmised Richard was in his room, moving about. They met in the dining-room, both perfectly dressed, both glancing critically at one another. There was no doubt about it, conceded Vicky, her husband was a man who always displayed refinement and cultivated taste, both in his day clothes and in those he wore now, for dinner. Vicky had decided to wear a black skirt and turquoise blouse trimmed with narrow black ribbon. She looked very young in the outfit, she knew, but she did not feel young. On the contrary, she seemed to have put on at least ten years during the past few days.

'Do you want a drink first?' he asked, his voice low and gentle. 'A glass of sherry?'

She shook her head.

'I'd rather have dinner at once, if you don't mind. I

want to change later and go over to see Father.'

'For any particular reason, Vicky?'

'Ought I to have a reason for going to see my father?'
She was not going to tell Richard that her father was
now under the doctor. He would probably be hoping that
he had a fatal attack, so that he, Richard, could come
into possession of even more money.

'No, certainly not. I'll come with you if you like?'

She hesitated, aware that if she went alone her father
might wonder at it and ask why her husband was not with
her.

'All right,' she agreed, and was surprised to see Richard's face brighten, just as if he had heard something
that pleased him.

It was past eleven o'clock when they got back to the
Manor. Vicky said a brief goodnight before running up
to her bedroom. She and Richard had been forced to act
with tenderness towards one another, and every time
Richard called her darling it was like the point of a
dagger piercing her heart. For herself the pretence had
been a strain of such weight that she now felt dragged
down by it. Slowly she undressed, took a shower, donned
her nightgown and was just brushing her hair when the
communicating door opened and her husband stood
there, his face dark with fury.

'Where were you this afternoon?' he demanded, meeting her startled gaze through the mirror of the dressing-
table.

Vicky pivoted on the stool, coming round to face him.

'Why should it interest you?' she asked almost in-
solently. She was still pent-up from the strain of posing
as the starry-eyed bride and she wanted only to get into
bed, switch off the light and be swept into oblivion.

'I do happen to be your husband,' he reminded her
harshly. 'Where were you? Tell me!' He advanced to-

wards her, a towering figure whose face was twisted with anger. She slid from the stool, making for the far side of the room, but moving backwards, an action that brought his teeth snapping together.

'It appears that you know where I was this afternoon,' she managed, though shakily. Is he going to murder me? she asked herself, aware that every nerve in her body was fluttering in unison with the palpitation of her heart. Never, during those idyllic days when she had believed herself to be a well-beloved wife, had she dreamed she would see her husband like this. 'What I don't understand, though, is how the information came to you?'

'You and he were having lunch together in the hotel! I've just had a telephone call from a friend of mine and the fact was mentioned, quite casually, that you were lunching with the young man who is surveying land around these parts.'

'What of it?' Vicky's voice was a little calmer now because she knew what she was going to say. 'If you can have a girl-friend then surely you won't object to my having a boy-friend? After all, it was only my money you were interested in, and you have that, haven't you?'

'By God, girl, you're goading me beyond endurance! Boy-friend, eh? Is that what he is?'

'He's my friend, yes! As I've pointed out, you have your girl-friend. I believe she's coming into a fortune within the next few months. Don't you wish you'd waited a little while longer, Richard? You could then have had your cake and eaten it, as the saying goes——' She got no further, her sentence ending abruptly as with a little cry of fear she tried to dodge out of her husband's way. He had leapt across the room, his face pale with fury, and now he gripped her shoulders, his fingers digging mercilessly into her flesh.

'I've warned you not to goad me!' he snarled, his face

so close to hers that she could feel his breath on her cheek. 'It was bad enough when you talked of that John Bailey, but to fling Louisa at me—I don't want her money! Get that!' He was obviously intending to thrust her into a big armchair but, his temper breaking all bonds of control, he pulled her to him again and shook her till she cried out, tears rolling down her face.

'Stop—oh, you're hurting me! Richard ...' She said no more, but resigned herself to endure the full force of his anger. And when at last he let her go she would have fallen had he not caught her by the arms again.

'I hate you,' she breathed. 'Yes, I hate you,' and in that moment she really believed she spoke the truth.

He held her, supporting her swaying body. There was no gentleness about him, no sign that he regretted his violence of a few moments ago.

'You said you'd decided to have the showdown because you didn't want to have a child of mine.' Richard spoke softly, half to himself, his glance flicking over her figure, arrogantly taking in the curves so clearly revealed through the transparency of the material of which her nightgown was made. 'And I seem to remember that you looked at me as if such a child would be tainted——'

'It would be tainted,' she flashed, her own anger rising above her fear now that his fury seemed to have died, 'tainted with the lust for money!'

For one terrifying moment there was silence and then, lifting her right off her feet, Richard looked down into a face totally drained of colour and said, his accents vibrating with fury and passion,

'You *will* have a child of mine—be it tainted or not!'

CHAPTER NINE

VICKY awoke after a restless night to find Richard was not beside her. She rose swiftly, as if by leaving the bed she could erase from her agonised mind the unbridled passion of her husband's mastery. She threw wide the curtains and opened the window, her brooding eyes moving from the gardens with their ancient trees, their statues and fountains, to the wild moorland beyond. Then she turned, to scan the room with its ponderous furniture. Yes, it was ponderous, but she hadn't really noticed before just how much it differed from what she herself would have designed. Here at Whitethorn Manor others had done the designing, she herself having merely made some small changes. At the bungalow all was her own creation, and the finished picture was one of beauty and good taste. If only she could put back the clock! Yet how many before her had said the same thing. It was a futile wish since what was done was done and there was no undoing it. No undoing . . .

Vicky's lovely eyes, pensive and sad, strayed to the communicating door. No sound came to tell her that Richard was moving about in his room, but she opened the door after knocking gently. There was an urgency about her that had come upon her unexpectedly. She knew that there could never be another night like the one that had passed. She was no slave to the lustful desires of a man whose love was given to another girl. She and Richard must talk, must try to find some way of separating without causing her father any pain. There must be a way! There *must*!

The room was empty and she listened, hoping Richard was in his bathroom. No sound. She happened to glance down at herself and was glad he was not there. She was dressed only in her nightgown, having forgotten to put on a housecoat, so urgent was her desire to talk things out with Richard.

After taking a bath and putting on a flared skirt of white cotton and a short-sleeved blouse of lime green, military-styled with epaulettes and two small flapped pockets, she brushed her hair, used the blusher to hide the intense whiteness of her cheeks, then went down to the morning-room. Richard was not there and it was clear that he had not yet had his breakfast. One of the maids heard Vicky and came in, asking respectfully if she was ready to have her breakfast.

'Mr Sherrand—where is he?' asked Vicky.

'He went out, madam, saying he would not trouble about breakfast.'

She found him ten minutes later, coming upon him unexpectedly as, having wandered into the more wooded part of the garden, she saw him sitting on a fallen tree, his head sunk in his hands. He was unaware of her presence and she stopped, halted by the picture of utter dejection he made. Her heart caught in spite of herself, since she felt certain that he was thinking of Louisa, the girl he should have married.

Vicky turned away, treading softly on the thick accumulation of bracken under her feet and avoiding any dead twigs which might, were she to step on them, disclose her presence.

Yes, they must part; there was no sense in their staying together, being unhappy. She fell to thinking of his tenderness towards her—though she could not have said why

—and almost against her will she was being confronted with incidents that proved beyond doubt that there was a good side to her husband. True, it was proved that he had married her for what her father could settle on him, but he had intended to keep the bargain he had made with Wallace: he would never let his wife know that he did not love her. Vicky pondered over his manner with her, and bewilderment became her dominating emotion. How could any man put up such a convincing pretence? She gave a sigh, having to admit that the simple answer to that question was that Richard *had* put up a convincing pretence; what was not so simple—and in fact it was totally illogical—was her conviction that Richard possessed a high degree of honour in that he had fully intended to treat her as a loving husband should.

Vicky wandered on, leaving the wooded part of the grounds and entering the more formal gardens surrounding the mansion. Her steps were automatic, though, her mind being fully occupied by the situation which she and Richard were in. He himself must have suffered agonies, married to one girl while loving another; he had been seeing Louisa in hospital and Vicky could imagine the eagerness of the meetings ... and the misery of the partings. Well, he could marry Louisa in the not-too-distant future ... For a while Vicky found herself fighting tears as the picture of Louisa, as Richard's wife, rose mercilessly before her mental vision, and it struck her that she could not stay in the vicinity of the Manor. Yet how could she ask Wallace to move out of that lovely house which he had obviously built for his retirement?

'What must I do?' she quivered, speaking quite audibly. 'Either I must stay with Richard or I must cause a major upheaval in Father's life.' Even had he been in perfect health she felt she would not have been able to ask him to move out of the bungalow; as things were it

was unthinkable that she should do so. Quite suddenly
she was calm, determined to do something positive, since
this indecision could not continue for ever. She would
neither stay with Richard nor ask her father to leave the
bungalow. For a long long time it would be agony, living
so close, inevitably seeing Richard and Louisa together,
but eventually the pain would ease, simply because there
was no disputing the fact that time healed.

Having reached the house Vicky found she had no
desire to enter its imposing porticoed entrance and she
walked on, taking the path leading to the lake. A little
rustic seat shaded from the bright morning sun by a mas-
sive copper beech tree offered peace and tranquillity,
and she sat down. But within little more than a minute
Kaliph came bounding along, Richard strolling along
behind him. Vicky decided they must talk at once, must
discuss their problem and try and resolve it.

He slackened his pace on seeing her there, then came
and stood looking down at her for a long moment, his
face an expressionless mask.

'I suppose,' he began stiffly, 'that I should apologise
for last night——'

'It's best forgotten,' interrupted Vicky, colouring up.
'There are more important matters for you and me to
discuss.' Automatically she moved to one end of the
seat. 'Have you the time now?' So calm, so composed
her attitude towards him; she had certainly grown up
since that fateful day when she had overheard the words
that had broken her heart.

'Important matters?' he frowned, ignoring her silent
invitation to sit down.

'Surely you must know that we have to talk? Please sit
down, Richard.' Her voice was as unemotional as her
manner, which amazed her, for deep within her the pain
was almost more than she could bear. To be near him

like this, loving him as she did, to be admitting that it would be heaven to feel his strong arms about her, his hard demanding lips taking possession of hers ... all this brought the burning tears to Vicky's eyes and she hastily turned aside, determined not to let him even suspect that she still had any love for him.

He sat down, his body erect, his profile taut. Was he still thinking about Louisa ...? Without preamble Vicky spoke, a stiffness in her tone that even to her own ears sounded unfriendly.

'We can't go on like this, Richard, I am sure you'll agree. So I've decided we must part—have a divorce.'

'A ... divorce,' he murmured, and it did seem to Vicky that his whole demeanour was one of relief. 'Because of last night——?'

'Because neither of us is happy,' she interrupted swiftly.

Richard turned to glance at her profile, saying, after a reflective moment,

'What about your father? You extracted a promise from me to the effect that this trouble should be kept from him.'

Vicky nodded, but immediately spoke of the idea that had come to her, in a flash, just a few seconds before he had come walking along the lakeside.

'I feel I could gradually pave the way by dropping him a hint now and then. You see,' she went on to explain, 'I've an idea that he might already be having some suspicions that our marriage isn't perfect.'

'You have?' Strangely, Richard was not revealing too much surprise at all over this piece of information.

'He bought me the horse because I'd been appearing depressed——'

'But at that time you hadn't discovered ...' He stopped,

having difficulty with his phrasing and Vicky finished the sentence for him.

'... the reason why you married me. No, I hadn't, but I'd been unhappy because you went out and left me. I didn't tell Father that you went out in the evenings, of course, but I must have given him the impression that I was not happy, because he mentioned it later, saying that there had been an occasion when he suspected I was not feeling as happy as I ought. I convinced him he was wrong,' she added, 'because at that time I was happy again.' She slanted him a glance, expecting he would question her about this but he remained silent, staring across to the far bank of the lake where two swans and their three fluffy brown cygnets were swimming about beneath a feathery cover of weeping willow trees whose branches were trailing the water. 'As I was saying,' she continued at length, 'I feel I can prepare Father for the divorce by dropping these hints. In this way he won't be too shocked when I finally tell him that the marriage has broken up.'

'You appear to have it all sorted out,' observed her husband tautly.

'I'm not willing to continue with this life. You'll be free to marry Louisa——'

'I want to talk about Louisa,' began Richard, but Vicky cut him short, unable to listen to anything at all about the girl her husband loved. And because she wanted to hit back, to prove to him that she too could have a future, she said coldly,

'And I would be free to marry too, if I wished.' The Labrador, standing with his head cocked, looking into the water, caught Vicky's attention at that moment and so she missed the scowl that fleetingly crossed her husband's face.

'You would marry again?' The element of disbelief in his voice brought two bright spots of angry colour to her face and caused her to flash at him instantly,

'Why not! I'm only young. Of course I shall marry again—and to a man who isn't interested in money!' Why she added this she would never know. She certainly had not meant to do so. It angered Richard, naturally, but he let it pass, asking if she had arranged to see John Bailey again.

'Because if you have,' he said between his teeth, 'you can cancel the date! While you *are* my wife you'll remember your position. I'll have no scandal attached to your name!'

Her eyes blazed.

'If you can have Louisa then I can have John! We discussed that last night!'

'There was no discussion. *You* made a statement.'

'What does it matter? You have her and therefore you've forfeited any rights you have over my affair with John. In fact, you've forfeited all your rights as a husband.' For a moment she paused, as if preparing him for her next words. 'If there's ever another night like last night then I shall go straight back to my father.' It was a brave statement, but she knew full well that she would never submit Wallace to a shock like that. Richard knew nothing of her father's illness, so he would obviously take her threat seriously. However, she was soon to learn that the threat was unnecessary, as Richard assured her there never would be another night like last night.

'You inflamed me,' he reminded her, and even now his temper flared, as if he were still half-blaming her for something he bitterly regretted. 'I warned you not to goad me.'

'Can we get back to the question of a divorce?' said Vicky. 'I expect you know how to go about it?'

'Seeing that I haven't had a divorce before—no, I don't know how to go about it.'

'Your solicitor will do everything,' she retorted, aware that he was being sarcastic, icily so, judging by his tone and the cold stare he gave her.

'I expect he will.' The Labrador was at Richard's knee again and he put out a hand to stroke his head. 'I haven't had your assurance that you'll not see John Bailey while you are still my wife.'

She gave a start of surprise,

'I thought that was settled,' she almost snapped, her desire being only to thrash out the matter of the divorce. 'I'm seeing John just whenever I like. You asked me if I'd made arrangements to meet him again and I have. We're going out to dinner at——' She stopped, deciding it would be more prudent to keep her husband in ignorance of the name of the hotel in Buxton where they were dining.

'When are you going out to dinner?' demanded Richard, his dark face almost evil in its expression. 'When and where!'

'That's no concern of yours. I don't ask where you meet Louisa. I know *when*, of course, because you're not at home,' she just had to say.

'It so happens that I am not with Louisa on every occasion when I'm away from home.'

'About the divorce,' she began, but Richard interrupted her, repeating his question about the date she had made with John. 'I shan't tell you, so you're wasting your time in asking me,' she told him firmly.

His eyes took on a glinting light.

'You do realise, Vicky, that there are ways and means of preventing you from meeting this man?'

'Are you intending to lock me up, Richard?'

'I could do just that,' came his cool rejoinder.

'You'd have my father to answer to!'

He gave an impatient sigh and there was a long and brooding silence as, absently, he fondled the Labrador's ears.

'Tell me,' he said, breaking the silence at last, 'didn't you ever suspect your father of encouraging me? After all, you knew of his ambition.'

Instead of answering his question Vicky put one of her own.

'How did *you* know of his ambition regarding me?'

'I guessed it from some stray remarks he made,' answered Richard, then repeated his question.

'The idea that Father regarded you as a likely husband for me did occur to me,' she admitted, 'but as he, like everyone else, knew you were almost engaged to Louisa I thought no more about it.'

Richard turned his head to look at her.

'If you knew I was almost engaged to Louisa then why weren't you puzzled by my interest in you?'

She averted her head, blushing painfully.

'I was vain enough to believe that I'd attracted you, and that you'd fallen out of love with her and in love with me.' Her voice caught, but he did not notice, as Kaliph began to bark at Cook's ginger cat as it came walking leisurely along the path.

He said after a thoughtful pause,

'You said you hated me. Was that true—or something said in anger, as retaliation?'

For one wildly optimistic moment Vicky thought she detected a hint of something significant in the question, calmly though it had been put. What would happen if she said no, she did not hate him? It very soon flashed upon her brain that she was trying to grasp at a straw that was not really there. The bald truth was that Richard loved

Louisa, and the sooner he was free to marry her the happier he would be.

A little flatly she said,

'No, it was not retaliation.'

'You really do hate me?'

'Yes,' she answered almost inaudibly, 'I do hate you.'

He drew a breath, turning his head as if interested in the two animals which were now facing one another, as if preparing for war.

'I can't blame you, even though there's so much you don't know.'

She was suddenly curious, recalling that this was the third or fourth time he had mentioned it.

'What is it I don't know?'

To her surprise he shrugged and said indifferently,

'It doesn't matter now. You're bent on this divorce, so there's no profit in my trying in any way to vindicate myself——'

'You can't vindicate yourself!'

'Not altogether, no. I'm entirely to blame for what I did. It was my decision and I can't blame anyone else for my action.'

Vicky saw by his expression that there was much he could tell her, yet she could not visualise any mitigating circumstances. He had by his own admission—when she had first had the showdown with him—married her in order to get himself out of financial difficulties, and also by his own admission he was in love with another girl at the time. How Louisa had taken the marriage was something Vicky would never know, but it was clear that Richard must have talked it over with her, explaining that if he did not take advantage of Wallace's offer then he would have to sell the estate. Was there a tragic, tearful parting? Suddenly Vicky rose from her seat, wanting only to get away from Richard and the knowledge that he was even now thinking about the girl and probably wondering just how long it would be before he could make her his wife.

'You're going?' he asked, looking up at her as she hesitated before moving away.

'Yes, there's nothing more to discuss, Richard. I shall give Father those hints I spoke of, and leave the rest to you. You'll see your solicitor?'

He nodded his head.

'If that's what you want, Vicky.'

'It's what we both want,' she frowned. 'You can't marry Louisa until you've got rid of me.'

'Don't put it that way!' he snapped.

'Not delicate enough for you? It's what we'd say in Lancashire. I've never been your equal socially, have I, Richard?' She looked down at his dark face, saw the grey tinge to his skin, the shadows in his eyes.

'I've never even hinted at such a thing! Where did you manage to get an idea like that?'

'It's the truth. I've accepted it from the start,' she told him in tones of quiet resignation. 'Our marriage would never have done even if we'd had a more favourable beginning.' And with that she would have walked away but Richard spoke quickly, reverting to John Bailey, asking again where she was meeting him, and when.

'I shan't have you seeing him,' he ended, bringing a militant light to her eyes.

'We've been into this, Richard. I go my way and you go yours.'

He stood up, tall and straight and overpowering.

'How far has this affair gone?' he demanded roughly. 'You haven't known him long enough to have fallen in love with him.'

How little he knew! She wondered what Richard

would have to say were she to tell him that she had fallen in love with *him* even before they had spoken to one another! Vicky had never made the confession but she had intended to do so, one day. That day would never dawn now.

'How long does one need?' she asked, unwilling to admit that she was not in love with John. Her pride demanded that Richard should believe she did care for him.

'I see,' stiffly and with suppressed fury. 'So you *are* in love with him. It didn't take you long, that's all I can say. He knows everything, so I expect he offered you sympathy?' The rough edge to his voice was now a rasp, grating on her nerves. It seemed impossible that this same voice had spoken so tenderly to her, had whispered endearments close to her heart as his body, strong and demanding, had possessed hers. Turning from him, she closed her eyes tightly, holding back the tears that strove for release. 'He knew, when he was here, a guest in my house, that I—I——' he broke off and once again Vicky finished the sentence for him.

'He knew that you married me for what my father gave you? Yes, of course he did!'

Richard's dark eyes roved her body, then settled on her face. She coloured angrily, aware that his whole attitude was one of condemnation.

'Did you not care what he might be thinking?' he asked, the tone of his voice matching the expression in his eyes.

'I never gave the matter a thought,' she answered curtly. 'To me it was only sensible to invite him to stay. He'd been lost on the moors for a long while, and in addition we'd been ages finding his car. It wouldn't have been very hospitable to have let him drive to Manchester after all that, and so late at night too.'

Richard said nothing; in fact, he appeared not to have been listening, so lacking in expression was his face at this moment. Vicky felt she should make another attempt to convince him that he could not prevent her from keeping her date with John but, sure that another argument would result, she wandered away, a little hurt that Kaliph made no move to follow her but, instead, sat down beside Richard who had taken possession of the seat again.

CHAPTER TEN

THE day of the show dawned bright, with the promise of a sunny afternoon. Richard, with Cutey in the horse-box, drove one of the Land-rovers used on the home farm, while Wallace drove Vicky in the Rolls. He had worn a rather odd expression when, having driven over to the Manor, he looked hard at his daughter when she appeared, spruce and spotless in her riding clothes. As they were driving to Handford he inquired hesitantly,

'Anything wrong, precious?'

She turned her head, her glance registering surprise, while her mind grasped the fact that here was an opportunity of dropping the first hint.

'What makes you ask a thing like that, Father?'

'I don't quite know,' he admitted, frowning. 'Maybe I'm worrying unnecessarily.'

'About what?' she prompted.

'Richard ...' A pause and then, 'He treats you well?'

'Of course.'

Wallace slanted her a glance.

'You're not the starry-eyed bride you once were, my darling.'

'It begins to wear off,' she told him, taking care to keep all emotion out of her voice. 'The honeymoon can't last for ever.'

He fell thoughtfully silent for a space before saying,

'It usually lasts longer than this.' Vicky said nothing and Wallace added, almost to himself, 'Your mother and

I would have had a lifelong honeymoon, had she not been taken from me.'

Vicky caught her breath on a little sob.

'Your love affair was exceptional, Father.'

'Nothing of the kind. Any two married people can remain in love if they try.'

'Try?' she echoed. 'No one should have to try.'

He drew a breath and to Vicky's relief said no more. The first seeds of doubt had been planted in his mind and more would come until, eventually, he would learn of the forthcoming separation and divorce.

'Remember what I said about giving a good account of yourself,' Wallace was saying later when Vicky, mounted on Cutey, was waiting for her event to come up. 'We'll be over there——' He pointed, but Vicky's eyes were on her husband, whose interest was undoubtedly fixed on another rider ... Louisa Austin.

Vicky's mouth tightened. She felt sure he was hoping that Louisa would win. Well, she would not win if she could help it, decided Vicky, leaning forward to pat Cutey's neck. The horse had done wonders in the practices, and she would do wonders today.

Vicky was soon watching the first competitor, Susan Ridgeway, who had been doing very well at the shows she had attended, but she had six faults and, happening to notice Louisa's expression as she watched Susan, smiling broadly and leaning forward to pat her horse, Vicky saw what could only be described as a smirk of satisfaction on Louisa's face. It was plain that Louisa had considered Susan to be her most important rival today.

Vicky's turn came before that of Louisa, and soon there was complete silence from the spectators, so superb was her performance with Cutey. She even surprised herself by gaining a clear round.

Louisa came next, her face taut with determination. She knew who Vicky was, of course, although they had never met. Nor had she ever seen Vicky before today. Richard would have told her that his wife was riding, though, so she knew that she was to have Vicky as one of her rivals for the coveted prize.

It was natural that Vicky's whole attention should be on the girl, and very soon she was frowning heavily as Louisa began to use the whip. Vicky had never even carried a whip. Cutey was her friend, not a defenceless animal to be driven beyond what it could perform with comparative ease and enjoyment. Vicky recalled Belinda's assertion that if the competition were keen then Louisa would drive herself hard—*and* the poor horse. She was certainly driving it hard now and it did not surprise Vicky when the horse refused. Swinging at the reins, Louisa reared her horse and prepared to take the jump again. Vicky turned away, feeling quite sick as Louisa's whip came down savagely on the horse's flanks. The crowd began to boo her as she came away, having totalled four faults.

Vicky was the winner; she rode round to a spate of cheering and clapping, leaning forward repeatedly to pat Cutey's neck as if she would remind the spectators that it was her horse's victory as well as hers. The crowd obviously understood because Vicky was gratified to hear, 'Good old Cutey!' being shouted from various places among the mass of people applauding the performance.

Naturally she was flushed as a result of her success, and as her eyes met those of her husband she saw only admiration, deep and sincere, in his gaze. He was glad she had won! Perhaps, like her, he had abhorred the use of the whip as Louisa, determined to beat Vicky, had driven her horse too hard. How could he be in love with such a girl was something she would never understand, thought Vicky, but perhaps it was the girl's beauty that attracted him.

'My girlie!' Wallace was saying as she dismounted. 'I knew it! Richard, aren't you proud of your wife?'

'Very proud,' was his immediate reply. 'Congratulations, Vicky.'

'Well, aren't you going to kiss her?' demanded Wallace.

'Of course.' Richard came forward, took hold of her arms, bent his head, and kissed her. She quivered at his touch and tears sprang to her eyes. She turned away, so that neither he nor her father should see that her eyes were suddenly far too bright. And it was only then that she saw John, standing some distance away, his whole attention on her. She smiled spontaneously and lifted a hand to wave. Richard, glancing over her head, set his mouth, while Wallace, looking round vaguely, asked his daughter who she was waving to.

'It's John,' she answered. 'A friend of mine. I'll beckon him to come over so that I can introduce you to him.'

Richard walked away! Vicky saw him go over to speak to Louisa.

'John, meet my father,' she was soon saying. 'Father—John Bailey.'

'How do you do?' Wallace examined the young man as if he were something he was intending to buy—at least, that was how John himself described it later, when for a brief moment he had an opportunity of whispering in Vicky's ear. 'And how, young man, do you come to be acquainted with my daughter?'

'John works for a firm you know, Father.' She mentioned the name, saw a frown come to Wallace's brow as he took another look at John.

'In what capacity?' he wanted to know.

John explained, but before he could go into even the

most minor details Vicky suggested they go and have some tea. She glanced around to find that both Richard and Louisa had disappeared. What would her father think? Vicky shrugged her shoulders; this would provide another little doubt in Wallace's mind regarding the success of her marriage. He was looking about, obviously searching for his son-in-law.

'Richard will probably join us in the marquee,' she said. 'Come on, for if we leave it much longer there'll be a queue.'

'But,' objected her father, 'it isn't the thing to go without Richard. How will he know where we are?'

'He'll guess,' returned Vicky lightly, aware that both Wallace and John were regarding her strangely. 'I don't think it's necessary to wait for him, Father.'

'If you say so.' Wallace was troubled and Vicky began to wish that her husband had not gone off and left them like that. She wanted her father to learn gradually of the failure of the marriage, not to have the knowledge thrust upon him so quickly that it could provide a shock which might have serious results where his health was concerned.

They had only just sat down at one of the tables in the marquee when Wallace was hailed and a lady appeared at his side.

'Mrs Basset!' exclaimed both Wallace and Vicky at once. 'How nice to see you,' added Wallace. 'I suppose you saw Vicky's excellent performance?'

'Indeed, I did! You were marvellous!'

The two men had risen to their feet and John was already offering Mrs Basset his chair.

'Oh, but I don't want to intrude,' she said. 'I merely came over to have a word with my old friend, and to congratulate his daughter. But thank you, young man, for——'

'Do join us, Mrs Basset,' invited Vicky just as her father opened his mouth to say something similar. 'We haven't seen you for ages.'

Mrs Basset accepted John's chair and he went off to find another.

'Not since your wedding, Vicky. Oh, but I shall never forget the lovely picture you made in that incredibly beautiful Paris model you were wearing!'

Vicky lowered her lashes, emotion sweeping over her as she remembered the dress ... and the day she had worn it. And mingling with her heartache was a great sadness that the vows made by Richard and herself were so soon to be broken.

Wallace was watching her closely; she joined in the conversation, not desiring that he should become too troubled about her. There was an odd expression on his face, an expression she had seen several times lately. Was he up to something? Vicky could not have said why the question came to her and she soon dismissed it from her mind, not thinking that Wallace might be contemplating having a word with her husband.

Mrs Basset was lively, her conversation intelligent, her laugh infectious. Vicky had never seen her father so free with a woman before. True, there had always been a sort of bond between him and Mrs Basset, but today there seemed to be something more. Instead of being wholly occupied with his daughter, Wallace had more interest in his old friend, it would seem. And when it was time for their departure Mrs Basset was a passenger in the Rolls, occupying the place by the driver, Vicky having insisted on sitting in the back.

Wallace followed the Land-Rover at first but later decided to pass it, being tired of the slow speed. Soon he had left his son-in-law far behind.

'What a magnificent placc!' exclaimed Mrs Basset as she got out of the car to have a look around. Although she had been at the wedding she had not seen Vicky's new home, as Vicky and her husband had naturally gone from the reception on their own, leaving the party to break up later. 'My, but you're a lucky girl, isn't she, Wallace?'

'Yes ... I suppose she is.'

'You always wanted to see her in a stately home, and you got your wish!'

'Are you coming in?' interposed Vicky swiftly. 'In fact, you and Father might as well stay for dinner.'

Wallace and his friend exchanged glances. To her great satisfaction Vicky heard her father say,

'Well, if you want us to, love . . .'

So it was settled, both Wallace and Mrs Basset expressing the hope that Richard would not mind that they hadn't changed.

'I'm sure he won't mind,' Vicky assured them, although she was wondering if her husband would consider them rather 'uncivilised' in dining in the clothes they had worn at the show. Vicky herself merely changed from her riding clothes into a short cotton dress and sandals. Let Richard think what he liked; he dared not voice his objections aloud, that was for sure!

When she came down she was surprised to find Mrs Basset on her own in the drawing-room, sipping the drink which Vicky had given her before going upstairs to change.

'Where's Father?' she asked in surprise.

'With Richard somewhere. Richard came back, walked in here looking rather tired, I thought. Wallace asked if I would mind being on my own for a while as he had something important to say to Richard.'

'Oh . . .' Vicky lost a little of her colour. Would Richard decide to tell Wallace everything? 'Are they in Richard's office?'

'I think they must have gone over to that summer-house,' said Mrs Basset, pointing. 'They went outside and strolled across the lawn. The next time I looked out of the window they'd disappeared.'

Vicky bit her lip, undecided as to whether she ought to go over to the summerhouse, but before she had time to make up her mind the butler knocked and entered with the information that there was a visitor to see her husband.

'A visitor?' repeated Vicky. 'Who——?'

'Where is Mr Sherrand, madam?' interrupted the butler, stolid-faced.

Mrs Basset, her interest caught, was watching the man closely, while Vicky, curious because of his expression, asked who the visitor was.

'My husband isn't about at the moment,' she added, aware of the start which Mrs Basset had given.

'The visitor is Mrs Sherrand,' said the butler resignedly. 'Shall I show her into the small drawing-room?'

'Mrs Sherrand?' repeated Mrs Basset before she had time to stop herself. '*This* is Mrs Sherrand!'

'It's Richard's stepmother,' explained Vicky, her heart thumping agaist her ribs, though why she did not know.

'Shall I show her into the small drawing-room?' repeated the butler, casting Mrs Basset a withering glance.

'Yes, please,' answered Vicky.

'I didn't know he had a stepmother,' commented Mrs Basset. 'What's she like?'

'I've never met her.' Vicky's eyes were concentrated on the view from the window. The summerhouse was over in a far corner of the garden, half hidden by trees and

flowering shrubs. 'I'd better go and find Richard——'
She turned. 'Please excuse me, Mrs Basset.'

'Of course, dear. Er—Vicky . . .'

'Yes?'

'You're upset about something?' No response from
Vicky. 'And you're not happy, either; I've known you
long enough to feel I can be outspoken——'

'Please,' broke in Vicky. 'It's nothing I can talk about.
In any case, I must fetch Richard.' And with that she
went swiftly to the door, opened it, and passed through.

She was crossing the hall when the voice reached her.

'So you're his wife!'

Vicky spun round to face the fair-haired woman
standing in the doorway of the room to which she had
just been shown.

'I'm Mrs Sherrand, yes,' she answered, unsuccessfully
trying to retain her composure. The woman's whole
manner was aggressive, from her piercing blue eyes and
tight-lipped mouth to the position she adopted with her
hands on her hips. 'I'm just going to find my husband.'

'Let me look at you! Daughter of a millionaire, eh?
All that money and yet I can't get what's my due!' The
words ended on a snarl of fury. 'Don't go away, young
woman; I want to talk to you!' The voice was loud;
Vicky glanced towards the room in which Mrs Basset
was waiting for Wallace's return.

'Kindly go back,' she said, lifting her chin. 'Whatever
your business is, it's my husband you want to see——'

'I was hoping to see you,' broke in the woman. 'Come
in here and we'll talk!'

Something in the woman's manner made Vicky obey.
She closed the door behind her after she and Mrs Sherrand had entered the small drawing-room. The woman
moved over to the fireplace, but Vicky remained just in-

side the door, regarding Mrs Sherrand warily.

'You might or might not know it, girl, but half this house and estate is mine!'

'Half——!' In a flash Vicky was hearing that part of Richard's telephone conversation where he had said, obviously in answer to a question put to him,

'Yes, you are entitled to half this——' and his words had been cut by an interruption from the other end of the line. She puckered her forehead in concentration as she tried to recapture something else of what was said. 'I have to accept it—I *have* accepted it, but these things take time. It's quite impossible for me to satisfy your ——' Another interruption ... Vicky recalled the look of hatred that had come to Richard's face, the way he had been so concerned in case his wife had heard any part of what he had been saying, his relief when Vicky had lied, telling him that she had heard nothing. That he had been speaking to his stepmother was a certainty, and Vicky decided she wanted to know as much about this woman as she could before Richard put in an appearance. Half the house and estate ... No wonder Richard had been troubled——

'What are you thinking about?' demanded Mrs Sherrand. 'Have you no comment to make on what I've said?'

'I was wondering how you could own half of this house and estate,' Vicky said in a quiet voice that was meant as an encouragement to Mrs Sherrand to come out with some further information.

'I'm James Sherrand's widow! He left me a pittance, and everything here to his son——' She swept a hand towards the window, indicating the acres of pastureland on which a magnificent Jersey herd grazed the lush green grass. 'But what he hadn't reckoned with was the law! I am entitled to my share—the solicitors have been thrashing it out for over two years and have at last reached an agreement. But will Richard pay? No, he's dallying, hoping I'll have died of old age before he's paid up.' The woman's face was twisted in a snarl. 'He got a fortune from your father, so why doesn't he pay up? Tell me, *why*!' Deep colour suffused the woman's cheeks; she was in such a fury that it would not have surprised Vicky if she had succumbed to a fit of some kind.

Vicky, pale of face and with her heart beating so wildly that it hurt, felt sickened that anyone could put such a value on mere money. Mrs Sherrand had sufficient to keep her in comparative luxury and yet she wanted more— wanted this estate carved up so that she would have another vast amount of money to squander.

'I have no idea why,' answered Vicky at last. 'I'm not in my husband's confidence as regards his business affairs.'

'Aren't you indeed! Well, your millionaire father is, obviously. I shall make it my business to see him—I know where he lives—and make *him* pay up——'

'Make my father pay you money,' broke in Vicky, eyes blazing. 'You'll do no such thing! Keep away from my father; he isn't well and I shall not have him upset—just you get that!'

'My, but you've a temper equal to that of your husband!'

'My father has nothing at all to do with your quarrel with Richard,' said Vicky more quietly. 'So you can leave him out of it.'

'He got Richard out of difficulty once and so why shouldn't he do it again? I'm having my share of this property while I'm young enough to enjoy it, so if your father doesn't pay up then it'll have to be sold so that I can have what's my right!'

'You've been pestering Richard for some time?' Before Vicky's mental vision now was her husband's drawn and tired countenance on so many occasions. She had come to the conclusion that he was desperately unhappy because of his love for Louisa, but now she was having other ideas ...

'Wouldn't you, in my place? Yes, of course I've been pestering him!'

'Threatening him?' said Vicky slowly and deliberately.

'If you like, yes!'

'With what?'

The woman's eyes glittered; she moved closer to Vicky. 'Who do you think you are, questioning me?'

'You yourself have brought me into it,' returned Vicky, amazed at her calm way of handling the situation, this after the rather frightened start she had made, 'and therefore you must expect me to ask you questions. I am suggesting,' she continued, 'that you threatened him with a court action?'

Mrs Sherrand's mouth curled in a sneer.

'How clever you are. Well, you're partly right, but the court case was not favoured altogether by my solicitor. He felt it was best not to antagonise my stepson too much. So I threatened to move in here——'

'Move in?' Vicky stared at her with something akin to horror. 'You couldn't do that!'

'What's to stop me? I'm the rightful mistress, and don't you forget it. I can move in just whenever I see fit.'

'I don't think you'd stay long,' Vicky could not help warning her.

'I'd be made uncomfortable? My good girl, you might believe that Richard could be objectionable to me, but anything he did would be mild compared with what I could do.'

Vicky could well believe it. She was thinking again of Richard's harassment by this dreadful woman, realising the reason for those sharp words he had used to her,

Vicky, almost certain that he had just shortly before been in touch with his stepmother, either by telephone or by receiving one of those letters of abuse she had heard him mention. She was talking again, in that loud voice that was almost coarse, saying that she fully intended seeing Vicky's father who, she felt sure, would advance at least some of the money owing to her.

'I've told you, keep my father out of this!' Vicky's own voice was raised now as she added, 'If you so much as go near my father's home you'll be thrown off the premises. I shall see to it that you are—by my father's two gardeners ...' Her voice trailed off and she spun round, alerted by the change of expression in Mrs Sherrand's eyes. 'Richard!'

He stood there, framed in the open doorway, Wallace close behind him.

'Your charming wife and I are just having a friendly chat, Richard,' remarked his stepmother, laughing.

Richard's eyes narrowed as he glanced at her across the room.

'What are you doing here?' he demanded.

'Oh, I've not come to settle in, not yet. Who's your little friend? I haven't met him before——' She let her eyes slide to Vicky. 'Your father?'

'Yes, and what about it?' Wallace was in the room, having brushed unceremoniously past his son-in-law, his whole manner one of aggressiveness. 'If you want trouble, woman, then you'll get it here! I've just been hearing all about you and your threats——'

'Wallace,' interrupted Richard quietly, 'this is my affair.'

'Be damned to that, Richard! We're a family and together we'll sort *her* out!'

'Father,' said Vicky, taking hold of his arm, 'come on, darling. Richard will deal with her.'

Richard's eyes met hers, a most odd expression in their depths.

'Your father and I have had a long talk, Vicky. I believe, when you've heard what he has to say, you'll not think quite so badly about me.' His voice had softened to tenderness; he was unaware of anyone else in the room as he added, 'I'm afraid I've broken the promise I made to you. Blame your father; he insisted on questioning me, and it was impossible to keep from him the fact that you wanted a ...' He glanced towards the chair where his stepmother was lounging against the cushions, a cigarette in a long holder now dangling from her lips. 'Talk to her, Wallace, while I settle this business. And then, if you haven't finished, I might take over?' A question as his gaze returned to his wife's flushed face. She nodded her head, confusion mingling with the staggering knowledge that her husband cared, that, whatever other reason he had had for marrying her, there had been love there as well.

'Yes, Richard,' she answered huskily, 'you—you might take over ...'

Ten minutes later Vicky had all the answers to the questions that had baffled her for so long. Her father took her into the library and there told her of his idea that Richard would make her a suitable husband. He had known that something was-wrong with his heart and desperately wanted her settled. He had met Richard several times when out walking and they had chatted together. Aware that Richard's finances were causing him grave anxiety, the result of his father's addiction to gambling and his stepmother's extravagance, Wallace had very carefully and subtly allowed one or two hints to escape him. He would be willing to help Richard financially. Richard had for a while ignored these hints, but, unhappy at the idea of losing his home, he had begun to consider the possibility of accepting Wallace's help. Wallace eventually told Richard that Vicky was in love with him; he also confided in Richard that he was desperate to see her settled, as he believed he had a heart complaint.

'Richard knew all the time?' broke in Vicky. 'You told him, but you didn't tell me?'

'We've been into that. There was nothing to be gained by worrying you with it.'

'But if anything had happened, look at the shock I'd have had,' she chided. 'Richard was preparing me when, that day, he said you were looking off colour.'

Wallace nodded, saying that Richard had thought it most unfair that Vicky was not being warned of what might happen. Wallace continued with his story, admitting that he was troubled about Louisa, as he did not know just how much Richard thought about her. He had reason to believe that the rumours of an engagement were by no means unfounded. Richard had told him that he cared for Louisa but, said Wallace, turning to slant his daughter a glance,

'I knew without any doubt at all that any man who married my darling child must very soon fall in love with her. So you see, pet, I wasn't cold-bloodedly marrying you off to a man who'd never love you, just to achieve my ambition.'

Vicky said nothing; she was impatient to hear more of the fascinating story. Much of it she had guessed, of course, but there was a totally different aspect, it would appear. Richard eventually decided to accept the help offered by Wallace, but only if he would accept the deeds of some land as security. 'But I'm over-running myself,' said Wallace, considering. 'Richard had met you, liked what he saw, and was in fact rather delighted when I phoned him to invite him over to dinner. After that the courtship went smoothly, with my child glowing with happiness and her old dad telling himself that his dream had almost come true. I knew that Richard, though he didn't tell me, had fallen in love with you and was, in fact, marrying you for love. But he was feeling guilty on two counts; Louisa, who later had an operation and was, so her father told Richard, losing her grip on life owing to the break with Richard, and you. He said that if ever you should learn the truth—that he had allowed me to help him—he wouldn't be able to look you in the face and lie.'

'You mean he would have to admit to marrying me for money?' Vicky was really angry with her husband, and it showed. 'That's exactly what he did do, when I tackled him——' She stopped, leaning away to look into her father's face. 'I suppose he's told you absolutely everything, while you were out there in the summer-house?'

'I believe so. I was as forceful as I usually am when I want anything. The lot! I told him, or else I was going right into the house to fetch you out there!'

She had to laugh, but she was still angry that Richard could blame himself so much that he could not say one word in his own defence. Wallace said it was the guilt complex, stronger in Richard because he was a man of honour.

'I tried to point out that he'd married you for love and not money, but he wouldn't have it.'

'How stupid!'

'Your husband, my dear, is above stupidity. His arrogance can appear without warning. It did, when I offered him some more money, as obviously the first lot wasn't anywhere near enough.'

'He said you were flaunting your money ...' Vicky spoke musingly, unaware she had voiced her thoughts aloud.

'Said that to me too, damn him! What does it matter when it's in the family? I said, but with that outsize guilt complex one couldn't make him see sense at all!'

'So for once you were beaten?' said Vicky, not without a hint of amusement. 'I'll bet that made you angry for a while.'

He let that pass, and returned to the subject of Louisa. She had asked for Richard to visit her in hospital and he did so, truly believing she was going into a decline or something! 'Well, off he went in the evenings——'

'When did he tell you this?' Vicky wanted to know.

'Just now, out there. We had a real heart-to-heart talk, I can tell you! I'd seen something was wrong and, by the devil, I intended to get to the bottom of it!' He came back to Louisa again, declaring that the girl was pulling Richard's leg. 'She wasn't all that ill at all! In fact, she was far from ill when she was on that horse today!'

'Richard was talking to her,' murmured Vicky, frowning.

'He was wild with you for being so nice to that fellow Bailey, so he went off to chat with his old flame. Served you right, I guess!'

Vicky bit her lip, recalling that she had gone out of her way to convince her husband that she was in love with John.

'Yes,' she sighed guiltily, 'it did serve me right.'

'When Richard spoke of your wanting a divorce— well, I couldn't believe it. Much as I love you, Vicky, I did advise Richard to give you a darned good spanking if ever you mentioned anything so stupid again!'

She coloured vividly, and it was at that moment that Richard appeared, his face a little drawn, but the expression in his eyes appeared to be one of relief.

'How did it go, lad?' Wallace left the sofa and stood by the window. 'A bitch, that, if ever there was one.'

Richard said, his eyes never leaving his wife's flushed face,

'The Manor's to be sold.'

'It is?' from Wallace unconcernedly. 'Well, we expected it, didn't we?' He seemed to be quite disproportionately happy at the news. 'Will you raise enough to pay her off? It's mortgaged up to the hilt, isn't it?'

Richard nodded, and walked over to stand with his back to the fireplace.

'Have you told Vicky everything?'

'I expect I've left some out. You'll get down to it eventually——' Wallace was moving towards the door. 'For the present, though, I'd not waste time on trifles. There must be other things you want to say to one another.' He had opened the door. 'So now the Manor's to go, and the whole estate, I take it that you'll come round to my way of thinking and take over my business? Oh, I know it's commerce and never shall the aristocracy tarnish their fair hands! Once it was like that, lad, but not now. Are you to become managing director of Fraser's? If not, I warn you. I'll wind it up and let it go!'

'That,' said Richard after a pause, 'would be a pity after you worked so hard to build up the firm.'

'You mean it!' Wallace stared for a moment, then burst out laughing. 'I knew it! When I want something I never fail to get it!' He glanced at his daughter, his merry brown eyes alight with triumph. 'It was hard work, because he was so stubborn, telling me in that haughty way he has that he wasn't intending to go deeper into my debt.'

'But,' frowned Vicky, 'you must have known that Richard was taking over, because I distinctly remember your saying that you were getting it ready to hand over to someone younger and more energetic.'

Wallace was taken aback, but soon recovered.

'I'd set my heart on his taking over,' he admitted, 'and

I've never failed yet, have I, love?' He went out without waiting for an answer, leaving Vicky alone with her husband.

'He's incorrigible!' she said, just for something to say, because she was dreadfully shy all at once, and guilty as well—this all mingling with excitement and the yearning to be in Richard's arms.

He remained where he was.

'I take it,' he said, 'that you never cared twopence for John Bailey?' So stern he seemed. Vicky felt very much like crying with sheer disappointment.

'You know I didn't.' She felt indignant suddenly and shot at him, 'Why didn't you tell me you'd married me for love?'

'Would you have believed me?'

She bit her lip.

'No—no,' she confessed, 'I suppose not.'

'You know now that I wasn't philandering with Louisa?'

She nodded dumbly.

'I should have trusted you,' she said meekly.

'And when I was out for whole days, I was sometimes visiting my solicitor, or else looking into various business propositions, desperately trying to salvage my home and other property.'

'I'm sorry ...'

'You once said sorry was no sort of a word to——'

'Please,' she broke in, tears misting her vision. 'I know I should have been more observant, should have known that you loved me ...'

For a long moment he said nothing, but stood there, his broad back to the fire, staring at his wife's bent head.

'Come here,' he ordered at last. Vicky obeyed, looking a little fearfully into his face.

'I—I——' She got no further as Richard, his austerity

falling from him, took her into his arms and, tilting her face with a gentle hand under her chin, kissed her quivering lips.

'It's all over, my darling.' He gave a deep sigh that seemed to rise from the very heart of him. 'I was convinced I'd lost you, Vicky, and the future looked so black that I was in despair! But I did try to find some way of keeping the Manor, knowing just how much you and Wallace wanted the status it gave. I had no intention of accepting any more money from your father and so, as I've just said, I began looking into other means of raising money.'

'I myself had never wanted a huge mansion,' confided Vicky, adding that it now appeared her father didn't either, he had shown so little concern on being informed that it was to be sold.

'He was too delighted at the idea of me taking over the management of the business,' Richard reminded her wryly. Then he added before she could speak, 'I shall salvage enough to repay him what he lent me; I'm convinced of that.'

'You should have told me it was only borrowed!' said Vicky indignantly. 'You condemned yourself unjustly!'

'Because the whole procedure was contrary to my principles right from the start. I very soon began to regard myself as the worst kind of fortune-hunter.'

Vicky looked accusingly at him.

'But you were no such thing! In reality you were intending to take good care of me, just as my father wanted.' Richard said nothing and Vicky went on to explain how his guilt complex had affected her, resulting in those little accesses of uneasiness she had known. She explained her feeling of inferiority, and this, combined with her uneasiness, had given her the impression that Richard was now regretting the marriage. 'There was definitely something missing from our marriage,' she ended, and Richard agreed, saying it could hardly be otherwise with all these misunderstandings.

'What I can't understand,' mused Vicky some time later, her mouth more rosy than ever from her husband's kisses, 'is why you didn't try to explain.'

'I wanted you to know that there was more than appeared on the surface and yet, paradoxically, I felt so guilty that I seemed to welcome your refusal to listen. It seemed to spare me the humiliation of trying to make excuses when I truly believed there were no excuses.'

Although all this was, to Vicky's mind, totally illogical, she let it pass without comment, going on to ask why Richard had said he loved Louisa at the time of his marriage to her, Vicky.

'I didn't say that——' He stopped, lifting a rather imperious hand to prevent the interruption his wife was about to make. 'Your memory, my love, doesn't serve you well. You asked me if, at the time of your father's *first putting the proposition to me*, I cared for Louisa. I answered yes.' He looked at her, holding her at arms' length, and shook his head a little admonishingly. 'I'd never marry one girl if I loved another, Vicky.'

She coloured at the rebuke. Knowing much more about her husband now, she was well aware that he would never marry one girl while loving another.

'I'm sorry,' was all she could find to say, hanging her head.

'I very soon fell in love with you, my darling,' he confessed. 'And you can picture my position then. I knew your father wanted you to be the mistress of a stately home, knew he was troubled about his heart. For me to marry you seemed the only sensible thing to do all around, since Wallace had assured me that you were in love with me just as I was with you. Yet how could I marry you without accepting your father's offer? I'd have had to say that the stately home would in all probability have to go—in fact, that the life your father had pictured for you would in the end be far less luxurious than what you'd been used to. Can you wonder, my darling, that I was in a dreadful quandary?'

Vicky nodded her head, wishing she had had some inkling of how he was suffering. She did recall that day when she had first met him ... and she had wanted to comfort him.

'I do think,' she murmured at last, 'that you should have told me you weren't in love with Louisa, because you must have known that I'd misunderstood your words, that I really believed you'd married me while loving her.'

'I tried, dearest, but as I've said, I had this terrible guilt complex. Added to that, I really believed our marriage was on the rocks, so there seemed nothing was to be gained by trying to make you understand.' He paused a moment, and she saw a glint of anger in his eyes. 'You'd said that you were no longer in love with me, and had in fact given me to understand that you cared for John Bailey.'

Vicky bit her lip, and again hung her head. Richard brought it up immediately, his fingers beneath her chin. The glint was still in his eyes as he said,

'Remind me to put you across my knee for that lie. Wallace has already advised me to beat you and I'm beginning to think that I shall have to take his advice.'

'Where shall we live?' put in Vicky hastily, her cheeks hot, the result of his threat. He was still forcing her head up, his gaze fixing hers. She saw his expression change, felt his lips on hers, so very tenderly, as he kissed her embarrassment away.

'That's for you to decide, my love. But first, I've some news that might afford you a tremendous amount of pleasure. Wallace hinted to me, when we were out there talking, that he and Mrs Basset might just make a go of living together. Neither of them has even looked at anyone since their respective spouses died, but now, it seems, they've both realised that they can give one another something worthwhile. I feel very sure we're to have a wedding in the family before the summer's out.'

Vicky's eyes were glowing. Nothing would please her more than for Wallace to marry his old friend. She asked again where she and Richard would live and was told that Richard and Wallace had discussed the possibility of building another bungalow not too far from the one already there.

'But the land's all being sold,' she pointed out, 'along with the Manor.'

To her surprise Richard was shaking his head.

'Not all the land will have to go. I'm keeping a fairly large acreage, so that your father's view can never be spoiled. I've had an offer from the Bowlangton Council who want the Manor for a home for deprived children— they'll be mainly orphans, from what I can gather. They want to keep the grounds as they are, and the home farm intact, as the older children will work on it. Most of the other farms will be sold to their present tenants, so there won't be any land available for building.' He paused a moment, his eyes faintly questioning. 'If the idea of the bungalow suits you, Vicky, we shall build not far from Wallace's.'

'I think it's a wonderful idea!' enthused Vicky, her eyes glowing. 'And to think that the Manor will be used for such a wonderful purpose! Oh, Richard, I think you've managed the whole affair very well indeed!'

'I'm glad it all satisfies you, my darling.' Richard drew her yielding body to him, crushing it in his embrace. Nor were his kisses quite so gentle either, since he was having the greatest difficulty in keeping his ardour within the rein he had put upon it.

'My beloved,' he said after a while, 'I rather think we ought to go in and see our guests, don't you?'

She laughed shakily, her own emotions heightened by her husband's passionate kisses.

'Yes, dearest Richard, I do think we ought to go and join them. They must be quite ravenous, waiting all this time for their dinner!'

Have you missed any of these best-selling Harlequin Romances?

By popular demand... to help complete your collection of Harlequin Romances

48 titles listed on the following pages...

Harlequin Reissues

Harlequin Reissues

Complete and mail this coupon today!

Harlequin Presents...

By popular demand...

24 original novels from this series—by 7 of the world's greatest romance authors.

These back issues have been out of print for some time. So don't miss out; order your copies now!

Harlequin Reader Service
ORDER FORM